# Pursuit

Also by Laurie Brady and published by Ginninderra Press
*Rummy*
*Rapport*
*Slices*

Laurie Brady

# Pursuit

## Humorous Stories

*Pursuit: Humorous Stories*
ISBN 978 1 76041 569 3
Copyright © text Laurie Brady 2018
Cover image: Pursuit of time. The missed opportunities © maxutov

First published 2018 by
**GINNINDERRA PRESS**
PO Box 3461 Port Adelaide 5015
www.ginninderrapress.com.au

# Contents

# Preface

Humour in literature springs from many different sources: the characters, the situations, and the nature of the author's expression. And it has many different forms: situational, farcical, satirical, burlesque, ironical and even the ridiculous. This probably accounts for why responses to humour are so variable. What appeals to one person may not have ready appeal to another.

Among some readers and critics there is a perception that humour, or certain types of humour, don't qualify as good or serious literature, not so much because they don't have artistic merit or universality, but because they don't provide the reader with the insights and understandings that good literature is supposed to impart.

But the purpose of humour is more than amusement or entertainment. Its most important characteristic is its incongruity, or some departure from convention or what is typically regarded as normal. This capacity, to highlight life's incongruities, enables humour to communicate powerful and often poignant messages about life. Arguably, the greatest expressions of humour are those that intimately blend laughter and tears, or amusement and insight.

The seventeen stories in this selection comprise all the expressions of humour mentioned above. Some appeal more readily to the emotions, and some to the intellect, but most of them, through the medium of incongruity, make powerful comments about the nature of the human condition.

# Doris

'Well, if you don't think your mother's birthday is important, that's a very sad state of affairs, and after all I've done for you.' The speaker was Doris Whittle, a fifty-seven-year-old mother of two girls, Felicity and Fiona, who lived by herself in the old liver-coloured family home on the outskirts of the city. Her husband had left years earlier, and while the two daughters enjoyed a relationship with him, they were loath to tell their mother, who blamed him for all the ills of her life.

'All the ills of the world in fact,' Fiona once said, immediately regretting it.

Both girls were married and had families of their own, so keeping contact with their father a secret proved difficult, though not impossible.

Doris had a post-menopausal bulkiness that seemed to add to her formidable bearing. She possessed slate-grey eyes that she liked to believe cut into the dissenting souls of those who challenged her but were in fact comfortably deflected. Her iron-grey hair was pulled tightly back across her scalp in the hope that it would smooth the wrinkles on her forehead, but nothing could disguise the deep furrow between her eyes that gave her the appearance of having both a permanent frown and grievance.

'Mum,' Felicity took up the challenge, 'we both told you three months ago that we were planning a trip to Europe. We said we'd ring you on your special day and celebrate with you when we got back.'

'If that's what you want to do, go right ahead,' Doris answered petulantly, not missing the chance to cast a fleeting look at the effect of her displeasure. 'Take your families and have a wonderful time, and don't worry about me. I'll go on working, and spend my birthday…' She deliberately left the rest unsaid. Sometimes the implicit was more telling.

'You know, Mum…' It was now Fiona's turn.

The daughters, after all the years, still tried an appeal to reason. It never really worked, but they still nursed a belief that it should at least be voiced. Its very utterance was an assertion of reasonableness, even if it fell on deaf ears.

'You know, Mum,' Fiona repeated, 'we've been planning this for a long time. The children are growing up fast and won't be interested in family holidays in a couple of years. You know Roger is stressed at work and needs a break, and Simon hasn't been well.'

'And I'm turning fifty-eight.' Doris stood her ground. 'Perhaps I didn't do enough for the two of you.'

The appeal to filial duty, sometimes a winner on previous occasions, was fuel for a smouldering fire. It had been used ad nauseam, and Felicity had her heart set on the trip. Her children were excited, and Roger had been prescribed a break on medical advice.

'Remember my Guides' camp,' she began stonily. 'On the Saturday, the visiting day, every kid except me had a mother there. You said you had to work, all that marking of assignments, but Mrs Small later let the cat out of the bag. You were at her place playing cards. And all those times when I did so well at athletics. You weren't working then, and could have come to watch and cheer me on like the other mothers, but there was always something more important – your cards, the art class, the hairdresser.' Felicity's voice rose in a crescendo.

Doris wasn't the crying type. Any attack was met, not with tears but with indignation, and sometimes counter-attack.

'What about my graduation?' Fiona, sensing that Felicity was heading for a points decision, resumed the offensive.

'What about it?' Doris interposed.

'You weren't there.' Fiona couldn't sustain the steeliness of her sister and began to cry.

'I had to work. You know that,' Doris said aggressively. 'I can't get the time off! I can't just walk out of the school!'

'You can, you can, you can,' Fiona, now being comforted by

Felicity, continued, adopting her more outspoken sister's anger. 'I rang the department, and they said you were entitled to parental leave when children graduate.'

Doris was furious. 'You mean to say you checked up on me?' But her indignation was tempered by having been exposed. Better to attempt another sortie. 'You know very well that I couldn't go because your father was there.' Immediately she felt confident that she was gaining the moral high ground. 'You obviously thought it preferable to invite that man, that poor excuse for a man who left us all and broke up this family, rather than your own mother.'

*

Pickett High, where Doris teaches maths, is a comprehensive coeducational school in a built-up suburb near a large shopping mall. Its position allows the teaching staff to leave the school to buy a selection of coffees at recess, though Doris usually buys her own without asking others, and is therefore rarely asked when someone else goes. In like fashion, when a teacher needs someone to replace them on playground duty, Doris is usually preoccupied.

She has therefore gained a reputation for not considering the needs of others. When a heated dispute arises between the teachers that threatens to derail the smooth running of the school, a teacher will be heard to say to another, 'For heaven's sake, Jenny, you're whittling,' or 'Stop doing a whittle,' and the humour often defuses a difficult situation. Of course, they are careful to see that Doris is not in earshot.

She is a good teacher, taking time to prepare and being diligent with her marking. Fiona believes that maths has particular appeal to her mother because it is not problematic like the other learning areas. There are definite rights and wrongs. She is a teacher of 'the old school' – full class, lockstep explanation, demonstration and practice, and teaching, like her personal life, is hedged with boundaries that define her commitment.

For instance, her senior class has two students who are brilliant at mathematics and, after external testing, were approached to enter a tournament of the minds to be held one weekend in the city. One stipulation was that the students participating had to be accompanied by their teacher. There were teachers willing to accompany the students, but the two had already entered the name of their teacher on an entry form, 'Ms D. Whittle', and a substitute teacher was not acceptable. Doris made it clear to staff and students alike that the weekends were her own.

In response to a question Doris asked the class about calculus, one student ignored the problem and asked if she would take Geoffrey and Lana to the tournament. Doris was angry and rebuked the student. The rest of the class was sullen except for a few unpleasant noises offered as protest that brought a titter of laughter. Phone calls from both of the student's parents, and a word from the principal, did not change her mind. 'I have something very important that weekend,' Doris said in defence, but when asked what, she declined to answer.

The following day, when Doris went for her lunchtime coffee, her car had disappeared from her usual parking spot directly outside the school. Could she have mistakenly parked somewhere else? She felt panic grip her. No, she distinctly remembered carrying the large box of Year Nine assignments from the car. She hurried to the school office.

'Stolen,' she managed to whisper. 'My car, my car. It's gone. Someone's stolen it.'

The principal and administrative assistant emerged from their offices as Doris's voice climbed beyond its normal volume.

'Are you sure?' the principal asked. 'Is it possible that you parked…'

'No!' Doris nearly shouted.

'Let's approach this calmly,' the principal tried to appease her. 'We'll go out and look. Mrs Squires will help too.'

'I told you already, it's gone.' Doris was exasperated and nearly called them fools. But as the principal and Mrs Squires headed out the door to the street, Doris followed, alternately running and walking in her agitation.

The principal knew better than to ask again where the car had been. He simply asked for its make, colour and number plate. It certainly wasn't there. Her usual spot was taken by another car.

'Mrs Squires,' the principal adopted his best soothing voice, the one he used to mediate fiery staff disputes, 'why don't you take Doris back and make her a cup of tea.'

Irked by being treated like an invalid or one of her Year Seven students, Doris nonetheless allowed Mrs Squires to take her back inside.

After several minutes, the principal returned looking solemn. 'I found it,' he said without apparent enthusiasm.

'Where, where on God's earth…' Doris jumped up spilling her tea, ignoring the principal's gravitas.

'It was a block down the street,' the principal explained, 'directly outside the mall, on the other side of the road and facing the wrong way, and between two parking spots in a two-hour zone. There's a parking ticket, at least I think that's what it is, or some sort of infringement notice on the windscreen.'

When Doris had raced away to retrieve her car, the principal couldn't help the smile he gave Mrs Squires, who struggled to suppress her own. And once the news spread throughout the school, the students were agog. There were grins throughout Doris's senior class, and the occasional nod to Mario, whose father owned the local garage, and who made up for his abysmal performance in maths with a talent for all things mechanical.

To Doris's disappointment, not sufficient was done to find the culprit.

*

'How can you eat this stuff?' Doris said to Miss Browne, who sat propped up in bed eating slowly and with great delicacy. 'It's sodden mash.'

Miss Browne waited till she'd finished her mouthful before she replied. 'It's not too bad, dear,' she said. 'Better than I get at home.'

'Hospital food's all the same,' Doris continued, 'and what with the charges, we should be wined and dined.' She pushed the tray away.

Doris had been admitted to hospital with a badly infected toe that had been caused by her stubbing it in her haste to retrieve her stolen car.

'We may have to lance it and drain the infection,' Dr Clark explained. 'It's a very minor procedure. Then antibiotics and some close monitoring.'

'What's wrong with this place?' Doris addressed the doctor accusingly. 'It took at least an hour to get a bed, and then only in a ward of four, and every doctor was busy. Blind Freddy knows I'm hurting. It must be obvious. I should be checked every hour, but where are the doctors, where are the nurses?'

Dr Clark had endured a hard day and, rather than adopt his best bedside manner, he walked away rolling his eyes.

The nursing sisters suffered the same treatment.

'People are hospitalised to get treatment,' she told a nurse, 'so where is it? You nurses are running to and fro like headless chooks, but no one's attending to my needs.'

The sister she'd chosen for her tirade was equal to the complaints, and undeterred by Doris's supposed piercing look. 'Ms Whittle,' she countered, 'there are people here who are dying, and your infected toe can hardly be compared. Mrs Luxton has very bad emphysema,' and she nodded towards a bed where a grey spectre of a woman was breathing oxygen through a mask. 'Miss Yen's very ill and her chemo isn't working, and Miss Browne, I see you've made her acquaintance, has a weak heart. So perhaps you need to consider how lucky you are before you start complaining again.' And she turned and hurried away. It was difficult to say who was the more indignant.

Dr Clark returned later that afternoon and pulled the curtain around her bed, ready to perform the minor procedure on her toe.

'No, you don't!' Doris was adamant, shaking her head as the doctor took out his syringe. 'I want to be knocked out when you do it. A general anaesthetic.'

Dr Clark, gritting his teeth, called for the sister and asked her to inquire if there was a bed in the day surgery for a very brief procedure.

Doris was awake when they wheeled her back to her bed after the surgery. Dr Clark asked for the sister to be present.

'Well, how did it go? You didn't botch it, did you?' Doris asked rudely.

Dr Clark was unusually benign. 'Sometimes, Mrs Whittle, we find that the infection is so bad, that amputation is the only solution,' he answered softly. 'If we don't amputate, the infection can spread, and more than the toe has to go. We have to make the decision when the patient is under the anaesthetic. Isn't that right, sister?' and he turned to the sister for support.

'Yes, I've seen a number of cases where that was the result,' the sister replied sombrely, while Doris sat numb, still woozy from the tiny dose of anaesthetic, and beyond words with shock.

'It all went well,' Dr Clark reassured the devastated Doris, and left with the sister. 'Well, we didn't say that we amputated her toe, did we?' he said.

'No, doctor,' and the sister smiled.

'You're my witness.' He returned her smile. 'Professional ethics and all that.'

Doris was very subdued. Her foot was heavily bandaged, so she assumed the big toe was gone. She was angry, but the anger wasn't focused. She was furious with Dr Clark but at the same time believed she could have been saved from something worse. It was the fault of the school, and the police, if they were ever called, for not apprehending whoever stole her car.

She rang Felicity and Fiona with the news that her foot had been amputated. They hurried to the hospital and were relieved to learn that it wasn't her whole foot at all.

The truth was only revealed when the sister came to her bed the following day. 'Time to dress that big toe,' she said breezily.

'But, but...' Doris spluttered when she saw that her toe was still there. The elation she felt was soon replaced with indignation. 'You told me I'd lost my toe,' she accused the sister. 'There'll be hell to pay for this!'

'I told you no such thing,' the sister counter-attacked, 'and neither did the doctor. He simply told you what could happen in cases like yours.'

'I'm sure...' Doris began, but battled to remember the exact wording, and lapsed into silence.

'I think you're mistaken,' the sister replied. 'People often imagine very peculiar things after an anaesthetic,' she said curtly and retreated.

'Do you think she's learned her lesson?' Dr Clark confided in the sister later that day.

'Hard to say,' the sister smiled. 'She hasn't been quite as vocal in whingeing, but she's still giving the nurses a hard time and hasn't a kind word for the pink ladies who have tried their best to help. It's still all about her.'

Throughout the next day, and just before her departure, Doris regained some of her more vocal indignation. 'You'd think my children might have been more often,' she told Miss Yen.

'But each of them has been here both days,' replied Miss Yen, who'd had no visitors.

'I can't wait to get home.' Doris changed tack. 'The food's rotten, the doctors deliberately mislead, and the level of care...'

She was interrupted by a shrill beeping, and nurses appeared from everywhere.

'It's cardiac arrest,' one called. 'Miss Browne in number one,' and a trolley soon appeared with two doctors running beside it.

One began working instantly, pressing and pounding Miss Browne's chest, while the other gave her an injection. This was all done as the trolley was being wheeled to the door. All else was silent. But as soon as the trolley passed the doorway, the piercing sound flatlined. Voices were raised, instructions called, and the trolley was raced along the corridor with doctors ministering to Miss Browne from both sides until the insistent noise that signals the worst of eventualities was absorbed in the silence.

The ward was hushed, deserted. A deathly pale Mrs Luxton bowed her head and crossed herself. Miss Yen cried quietly. Both no doubt were thinking of their own uncertain future.

And in that funereal place that Miss Browne had once occupied, a strident voice bawled out, 'Has no one thought of me!'

# Graduation

They arrive for their moment of glory on the stage, the fruits of the years, and rite of passage to a brave new world, these fresh inheritors of promise, cosmetic and assured, their hugging dresses and toothpaste smiles knotting my emotions and leaving me feeling as old as the university's sandstone, and no more malleable. It's graduation day for the teacher education students, mainly girls, and the lecturers who comprise the academic procession are gathering outside the hall where the latecoming students are still entering for their appointed seats.

They look polished and mature, Eliza Doolittle transformations, so different from the once-perennial students in their tatty jeans and sweatshirts, most of whom I've known for the four years of their degree. And every year, surprised by the metamorphosis, I have to admit that I'm no Henry Higgins. I've taught them about their profession, but deserve no kudos for their emergence as impressive men and women. Time and nature must take the credit.

It's ten o'clock. The time has come. A bell rings from inside the hall. We're ushered into two lines, each of us is given a particular place, and instructions about which way to turn when we reach the steps to the stage. I make sure the tassel is hanging to the right on my trencher. The chancellor, dean, guest speaker and official party bring up the rear, so that they will be sitting at the front once the procession fills the stage from the rear. The mace bearer leads the way, holding a ceremonial brass staff high in front of him. This is the church of scholarly pursuits.

'Quick. We're on our way,' someone whispers.

We hush and the sounds of 'Gaudeamus' float from the hall, this time pre-recorded. For some years there's been a choir, but not today. We begin the slow walk down the centre aisle, two by two.

At this stage every year, I feel prankish. It must be something about the starchy formality, the expected solemnity, the old-world regalia of coloured gowns, braid and silly hats that I'm tempted to flout. Perhaps it's the costume that separates us from the rest of the world, attire that screams status, or some hierarchy of importance that's an anachronism in the modern world. If my companion in the other line is female, I contemplate taking her hand, imagine skipping up the aisle like two infant children entering the classroom. It seems the natural thing to do.

I sometimes imagine myself as a court jester, donned in gaudy red breeches and hose, and a three-pointed cloth hat with a jingle bell at each point, perhaps a hat resembling the ears of an ass. Or a buffoon like Malvolio in yellow stockings and cross-gartered. I smile at the faces that turn to watch our entry, acknowledge the familiar among them with a nod. Others in the procession stare fixedly ahead, or perhaps they're just bored.

We climb the steps, Browne goes the wrong way as he has done for the last twenty years, and we stand in front of our seats. Fourth to the right, I recall. Second row. A robust nationhood's appeased by the national anthem, again piped through speakers and sung heartily, and there's the customary acknowledgement of our forbears who spread their wisdom on the land. Pre-attention coughs subside, the wings of programs hush like birds in flight, there's a gravid pause, and the chancellor walks to the rostrum and begins. We sit in unison, and some remove their trenchers to be nursed throughout the proceedings.

The guest speaker carries the weight of his degrees, fellowships, publications and research grants together with a ream of notes to the rostrum, and starts with the traditional congratulations to students, not forgetting the long-suffering parents and noble academic staff. Someone passes wind. Smiles are suppressed. People look at Browne. We settle in for the long haul.

I see Debra in the fourth row, all *Vogue*, her usual animation subdued by elegance. Debra Manning. Recall the time two years ago she collided with me as she ran to another class, her apology infected by an impish laugh. See her down on all fours with me to help gather my scattered notes, her hand resting without a hint of self-consciousness on my arm, our rush of pacifying talk followed by laughter. I think then and now of her headlong charge at life that for a moment carried me beyond my own perorating lean on rostrums to the message in her eyes.

Remember her final year, a forgettable one for me. 'I've heard…' she came to my room to say, and that was all, before the sudden kiss beside my mouth, lingering a little, I think, certainly a wet and warm taste of peppermint. 'And if…' Again the rest was assumed or better left unsaid, and for a dangerous moment, heart and mind conspired.

'And so I congratulate you all again. You are our future leaders. We entrust to you the education of the emerging generation in this time of great change and uncertainty. Never has education been as important as it is now. As you go from this protective environment that has nurtured and supported you, into the world beyond, remember…'

Déjà vu. How many years have I walked up that aisle in different processions and sat here, looking out on a sea of fresh student faces, to hear the familiar advice? How many thousands of students have I clapped as they walked, ran or stumbled across the stage, plunging into other lives, and leaving this cloistered one behind? How often have I indulged the pleasure of helping a student achieve, or enjoyed the compliments, the laughter and the good-natured ribbing, even the not-so covert affection? What was her name, the one that called me 'boofhead', and laughed, reaching out to me? I laughed too after feigning hurt pride.

There were scary times too, like a girl called Christine something, phoning me late one night, how she got my number I still don't know, and when I pressed her about why the urgency for a meeting, claimed that she believed I was the father of her *in vitro* child. Taken aback, I explained that I'd never made the necessary donation, so it couldn't possibly be me, and early the next day contacted the counsellor, who revealed some time later that Christine was receiving treatment for schizophrenia. Imagine the repercussions if her belief had been spread about the campus.

The address came to an end, and the vice chancellor took his place at the rostrum for the vote of thanks, prepared rather than reactive. 'Please thank our speaker for an inspiring address, so appropriate for the times, an address that gives us all, particularly the graduating students, food for thought...'

The awarding of degrees follows. The dean strides to a side microphone to read the names. He's rehearsed the foreign-sounding ones. There's a doctorate, several masters degrees, but mainly bachelors in teaching. An administrative assistant stands by a table to ensure the chancellor receives the correct script to present. The graduating students climb the steps and approach stage right, lift their trenchers in salute, then walk to meet the chancellor in the middle of the stage and are given their degrees before leaving stage left to resume their appointed seats.

'Virginia Constance Abbott,' the dean intones.

With head locked upright, and carrying a nervous smile, Virginia approaches carefully as if the imagined deportment book might fall from her head and mock her balance. As the first, she knows she is likely to excite more interest than the hundredth student. Hoisted on toes by black stiletto heels, she climbs the steps to the stage, a crablike ascent in thigh-shackling black, minidress on maxi behind. Reaching the top, she trips before she can doff her trencher to the chancellor, and takes her certificate on the run, impatient for scholastic glory.

'Mary Heather Anthill.'

The long procession has begun. Some stride purposefully across the stage, smiling, and reach for the chancellor's hand with the full quota of assurance. Some walk slowly and casually, as if in protest against assembly-line haste. The timid hurry across with heads down like scared rabbits, not comfortable with the fleeting glory. Only a couple are dressed in the usual student garb, having misunderstood or ignored the significance of the occasion.

A few of the popular students earn whistles and hoots to supplement the polite applause. The lapse in protocol is ignored. A few of us clap every student. Some fairy clap or tap their laps with their programs in approbation. Others don't bother at all. The chancellor holds a few students in conversation, but never for more than a few seconds. A university photographer stands to the far left to snap the students as they leave the stage.

'Debra Joyce Manning.'

She's in the first category of purposeful, smiling and assured students, and I find myself hoping that she might turn as she begins her walk to acknowledge me. But that's a tall order as the whole procedure only takes a few seconds, and it would be obvious to all assembled on the stage. I chastise myself for my self-centredness.

As the procession continues, and the lecturers wearily keep an eye out for Sophie Zlatos, the last student in line, who keeps edging closer to the stage, I hear my own name read out by the dean.

Taken by surprise, I quickly stand, shed my mulberry gown and hood with flare, and to the accompaniment of some raunchy music, divest myself of all my clothes. They come away easily in a few seconds without the usual tug at socks and fumbling with shirt and fly buttons.

I'm greeted by wild applause from the grateful audience as I stand naked, except for the trencher on my head. Then with my best prognathous look and simian lope, I prance about the stage, beating my breast with both fists, grasping my genitals and directing a grunt and a growl through the dean's microphone.

A catch-me-if-you-can game ensues with the vice chancellor and dean in pursuit, as I run down the centre aisle, circle the back of the hall, and run back up the side aisle to the stage. Someone throws flowers. Security is summoned and I'm eventually held and draped with my discarded robe. The students are cheering and my capture is greeted with boos from the auditorium.

But as I'm led away, flamboyant Jacqui Flannagan, the lecturer in Art emerges from the back row, already pinkly nude with pendulous breasts swaying, and, assuming centre stage, begins to karaoke 'Bodyguard'. The dean and vice chancellor, jealous of the acclaim I received, or perhaps craving the same lack of inhibition, strip naked, and form a backing duo for Jacqui, swinging in tempo, with arms interlinked, and singing in perfect harmony. Soon the students are all standing in their front row seats and singing along, waving their beribboned degrees in the air: 'I, I, I, I, I will always love you.'

'What are you smiling about?' my companion in the adjoining line asks as the procession stands to depart. 'You're miles away. What's the joke? Don't forget your trencher.'

'It's the only thing I'm not likely to forget,' I tell him.

The audience remains standing as we depart, just as they did when we entered, so I'm able to scan the faces of the students, trying to read the mix of emotions that a concluding chapter of life inevitably brings. I wonder if their pleasure is tempered by a little sadness. Like mine, I suppose. Some of them look at me curiously.

The audience follows the students, who follow the procession from the hall. Once outside the door, we disband, moving in all directions. Students search for parents and, once found in the throng, some of them are introduced.

'I've heard so much about you,' they say. 'We get a rundown of what you say in your lectures. Thank you so much for all you've done.'

Students queue for the commercial photographers, and the framing of their degrees. My waxing testimonials from favoured students segue to master and apprentice photographs with both of us in full regalia. Sometimes I'm hugged, aware of the softness of their shoulders against my arm. There's even the occasional peck on the cheek. And yet my 'Let me know if I can…' trails away, lost in competing demands. Their world is too big an oyster now.

Half an hour later, the hall is almost empty, and crumbs remain from sandwiches and cakes where polystyrene cups have glued coffee rings on paper tablecloths laid on the tables spread about the foyer where morning tea was served. The cleaning staff is already at work.

There's another graduation this afternoon. Many parents are rewarding their sons or daughters with a celebratory lunch.

Debra is leaving with her family, a young-looking mother and father, a little sister, and what is certainly a boyfriend, not the type you'd expect. They never are. She waves from a distance, and is gone, our scattered meanings left untouched, another inheritor of promise in a daring world where new realities seduce, and old allegiances must wilt and die.

# Antidote

How often does a defining statement come completely out of the blue? 'I love you,' anxiously rehearsed by one, might be bewildering for the other, and might herald a wonderful future, or it might threaten a friendship that has been sustained in precarious balance. The very suddenness of 'I've been offered a job in Cambodia,' would have to cause a serious re-reckoning for all affected by the move. Life fires challenges like these at point-blank range.

It was like this for Ellen Tompkins, a forty-three-year-old stenographer from Croydon Park, a suburb of Sydney. Ellen lived with her husband Ted and two teenage children in a typical suburb in a typical street in a typical triple-fronted red-brick house next to a park where the children had played until swings, see-saws and slippery dips were replaced by iPhones, the internet and the lure of the opposite sex. Life was good. She had kept a close circle of old school friends, the boss had promised her a promotion, Ted was attentive between his forays onto the golf course, and the children's hormones were in remission.

It came from nothing. A non sequitur in their mealtime conversation. 'This marriage possesses too much lust.' Silence. More silence.

'I beg your pardon,' Ellen finally remarked, turning to Ted, who had put down his knife and fork from eating his bacon and eggs.

'This marriage possesses too much lust,' Ted repeated, fixing Ellen with an intent look that seemed to demand confirmation, or defy opposition.

'Do you really think so?' was all a shocked Ellen could manage. But the look Ted gave her left no doubt about his conviction.

'It has to go, Ellen,' he said resolutely.

'All of it? Do you think we could keep just a little of it?' Ellen suggested. 'You never know when we might need it.'

'No,' Ted replied. 'The children might stumble over it. It might even infect the cat.'

'What if we store it in the attic, the cupboard under the stairs, or lock it in the tool room?' Ellen coaxed, but she met with the same answer.

Ellen knew her husband better than to argue. A reasonable approach would normally be to suggest delaying the decision for a day and revisiting it after sober thought. But once Ted had made up his mind, there was no room for negotiation. It was better to be compliant, particularly now, because this could be a symptom of far more serious things. Perhaps the whole marriage was under threat.

'The lust has to go,' he said again peremptorily. 'We'll start tomorrow. Both of us can probably finish it in a day.'

*

They started early, waiting only for the children to leave the house for their stay-overs. They wouldn't attempt such a task if the children were present, as they would certainly query, perhaps even be excited by, the prodigious amount of lust uncovered in the house, and be even more suspicious of its removal.

The bedroom contained the most. The bed, the grandmother chair and even the walk-in robe were thick with it. Ted remained grim-faced throughout the removal. The dining, lounge and kitchen needed thorough investigation. Behind the cushions on the three-seater lounge the lust was prolific. It was even under the lid of the piano. Ellen was startled to find some in her daughter's bedroom, but thought better of telling Ted.

It took them most of the day, and by mid-afternoon, Ted seemed more at ease, and started to chat and even joke with Ellen. 'I saw you hide that bit under your sweater and put it in the cupboard under the stairs.'

'I've got a lot stashed away,' Ellen parried, and they both laughed.

They brought the otto bins to the back door, and disposed of the lust among the vegetable scraps. There was soft lust, perforated lust, feathered lust, crystalline lust, there was lust that was wet, friable, corrugated, slippery, sharp, furrowed, brittle, perfumed, furry, pimpled, icy, varnished, melting, rubbery, polka-dotted, steaming, frothy, pliable, stitched, shredded, beribboned, tensile, coiled, diaphanous, gelatinous and sequined. It all went in the bin.

'Well, that's a job well done,' Ted proclaimed, rubbing his hands with satisfaction.

\*

The storm arrived in the early hours of the morning. They were awakened by the shrill wind and the rain beating against the windows. The branches of an old tree knuckled the eaves. Ted, grumbling, donned his dressing gown and checked to see if the windows and glass doors to the patio were secure.

Ellen's first thoughts were of her children.

'I'm sure they'll be just as safe with the Hamiltons and Brands as they are here,' Ted reassured her.

Morning allowed a fuller appraisal of possible damage. Two terracotta pots on the patio had blown over and disgorged their camellias and mounds of soil, and a little water had leaked under the door and onto the tiles. Nothing serious. But an hour later, when Ted ventured outside, he discovered that the otto bins left on the nature strip outside, were lying on their side, the lids were open, and the contents, except for a few rancid vegetable scraps, were gone, washed away through the park and down the gutters to who knows where. The lust was gone, and two dogs with mange and bared teeth were fighting over the remaining evidence of their labours – a piece of gelatinous lust.

\*

Peering from the window of the breakfast room an hour later, Ted saw at least fifty dogs in the park next door. There were Irish wolfhounds, Gordon setters, Maltese terriers, Rhodesian ridgebacks, beagles, kelpies, Jack Russells, chihuahuas, Labradors, Great Danes, poodles and numerous that couldn't be identified by breed. It could have been a judging for best dog at the Royal Easter Show, except there were no owners present, and their behaviour, or presentation, far from being immaculate, was obscene!

Ted was outraged. This can't be allowed to happen, he thought to himself, particularly when the neighbourhood is full of children, and, knowing that dogs did not like being sprayed with water, he went next door to the widow Hastings's place to borrow a garden hose, hoping that this might cool their ardour and disperse them.

Beryl Hastings was a large and corpulent late middle-aged woman with a perpetually red face that looked like a severe case of sunburn, and with two missing front teeth that drew the fascinated attention of listeners to her imagined exploits. She had always been particularly attentive to Ted. Ellen and the two children had noticed this and ribbed him about it. 'Beryl's waiting for you next door, Dad,' his daughter would tease when there was a dispute over what television channel to watch.

'The dogs…' Ted began, and nodded towards the park when Beryl had opened the door. 'I wonder if I could borrow your hose.' He kept his eyes averted, hoping the reason was sufficiently apparent, because to be more explicit would prove embarrassing.

Beryl took in the scene at a glance, and turning to Ted she smiled suggestively. 'Mine's out of action right now,' she explained quickly, 'but surely yours is adequate,' and she gave him a lecherous look and rubbed her enormous breasts suggestively.

Escaping the widow's now groping hands, Ted rang the fire brigade. They were only a block away, and while there was no fire, Ted believed the situation should at least be regarded as morally inflammatory, and deserving of public service. But the answering machine reported that the staff had only just called in sick.

'What, all of them?' Ted shouted into the phone in frustration, as though someone at the other end might hear him.

His final stop was Tom Eustace, who lived only a few doors away, and was the suburb's vet. He was a young man who'd been in Croydon Park for three years now, and was popular with the locals. Perhaps he'll know what can be done with the dogs, Ted reasoned. That's his stock in trade after all. Ted was about to knock on the side door that opened onto the treatment room, when he noticed the sign taped to the door, 'I'm tending an animal much in need,' and he heard a protracted groan.

That's it, Ted said to himself. That's it! See if I care. But of course he did. He would go home and lock himself in the study. At least that room was on the other side of the house to the park. Out of sight, out of mind. Let someone else be the custodian of public morals!

*

Phil Evans lived a few blocks away from Ted. He was a real estate agent with an established firm, and had a reputation for at least not inflating the price that the vendor might obtain in order to get the sale. He was a spare and wiry man who was married to one of Ellen's old school friends. Apart from the odd family socials, Ted met Phil on the golf course, where they often played as a foursome and, having similar handicaps, they were very competitive.

As Ted turned onto the path outside the vet's house, he collided with Phil and sent him sprawling. Phil quickly regained his feet while Ted clutched at his shin. It was no one's fault. Neither of them had been looking where they were going.

'How are you, Ted? Are you hurt?' Phil was unusually indulgent. 'I'm so sorry. It was my fault. I wasn't thinking. That'll teach me for having my head in the clouds.'

Ted watched his friend with growing alarm.

'Can you forgive me?' Phil continued, unusually contrite. Unusual because Phil wasn't normally someone who admitted to fault. Several times on the golf course, while selecting the putter from his bag, Ted had turned back to find Phil's ball on the green a metre closer to the hole than where it had landed. Once, he had actually seen Phil nudge it forward with the toe of his boot but, when challenged, Phil had vehemently denied it. That had soured the rest of the afternoon.

'No, I'm not hurt, just a bump on the leg. It was no more your fault than mine,' Ted responded, and feeling that something was amiss, he asked more gently, 'What's going on, Phil? Is something wrong?'

Phil's face contorted, and he clutched at the mess of remaining hair on his balding head. 'A terrible thing has happened,' he barely murmured, responding to Ted's compassion, and stalled.

'What is it, mate?' Ted was more solicitous now. 'If there's anything I can do…'

The burden of grief was too great for Phil to contain any longer, and the words came in a haemorrhage. 'I was carrying a large sack of guilt to St Johns. There were all sorts of guilt in the sack, juicy, smooth, metallic, buttery, dense…but it was so heavy, and you know I'm not strong,' he wailed, 'though I didn't have to be – strong, I mean – I could manage quite well, but then more rain, and the wretched wind came, awful wind, and it burst, the sack tore apart, and,' he was nearly sobbing now, 'it was scattered to the four winds. I could see it all disappear, and there was nothing I could do. Please forgive me. Forgive me for I have sinned.'

\*

Ted reassured his mate, explaining that some good could well come of it, that some people, who needed a little chastening, might become more contrite as a result. And swearing him to secrecy, he told Phil about the lust. 'Besides,' he tried to instil some optimism, 'it wasn't anything like that time a year ago, when that woman spilt a suitcase full of aggression while having coffee at Gloria Jeans.'

As he was returning home, the clouds moved away like a pulled curtain, and the sun suddenly emerged, bathing him in warmth and turning the wet and drab greys into rich colour. The dogs were leaving the park with no spring in their step, the Great Dane with the Labrador, the poodle with the Maltese terrier, the Irish wolfhound with the Rhodesian ridgeback, all looking forlorn, with their tails between their legs.

He could hear his children's voices laughing inside the house. Is there anything more delicious, more gratifying than that, he told himself. It was sheer music. And pinned to the front gate, sealed in an unmarked envelope, was a letter from Beryl Hastings, 'Im so sooo sorry for what I done. I hope we be friends all-ways.'

# Audling

'Eureka! I've got it. I've found the answer.'

Several of the restaurant's customers looked around curiously as Rupert's fist banged the table with exhilaration.

'What, here,' Liam laughed, 'between the soup and the macaroni?'

'Some ideas, or half-formed ideas take a while to incubate,' Rupert answered distractedly, and began to scribble frenziedly on the paper table covering.

Rupert Tanner was a postgraduate student at Bligh University, in his third year of studying for a doctorate in the philosophy faculty. He had a small teaching load as a tutor of undergraduate students. Confident, and socially adept, except when his mind was dealing with some weighty theoretical issue that locked out the rest of the world and just about everyone in it, Rupert, even from his schooldays, unassumingly wore the tag of 'the one most likely to succeed', a label that owed as much to his good looks as to his intelligence.

'Thanks for the scintillating company, mate,' Liam joked three-quarters of an hour later, as he called for the bill, and as Rupert was removing the table's paper covering, now full of tiny script and symbols, with arrows in all directions, and asterisks. 'He's just found the answer to the world's ills,' Liam told the amused girl who returned with the change.

The next day, at the weekly faculty meeting, the dean announced to the staff, disguising his excitement behind a mask of scholarly solemnity, that Rupert had made an earth-shattering breakthrough in his doctoral studies.

'I don't want to pre-empt,' he warned, 'because as academics, it's important that any new proposition is subjected to the most rigorous examination before it is brought to light, but,' he paused for effect, 'we may have reason to believe that this will bring great credit to Bligh.'

Rupert was surprised, even uneasy, believing that such a compliment was over the top.

Later that afternoon, Rupert received calls from two professors at other universities in the state.

One seemed to be exaggeratedly casual. 'I've read some of your early work in the journals,' he said. 'Interesting. You must have come a long way. If there's anything you'd like to discuss with me, I'll be in your neck of the woods tomorrow...'

The other was more direct. 'So what's this I'm hearing, something about the solution to the problems of the world?'

If these calls caused some consternation, it was nothing in comparison to the chain of events that would follow the headlines and photographs of him in the following morning's *City Gazette*:

'Young Bligh University researcher discovers the ultimate philosophy – the answer to the perils that confront us all.'

*The Bligh Telegraph* that evening was even more colourful in reporting, 'The universal questions on belief and emotion, love, religion, life itself, the questions hotly disputed in every tongue since human time began, from boardroom to bar, from lecture room to car back seat, all answered by our own Bligh genius. The eager world awaits revelation.'

There was a small tinge of pride, especially when he was aware of the people nodding in his direction on the bus trip to work, but that vanity soon disappeared, and the unwarranted attention he was receiving aggravated his concern for the probable repercussions. Where had it all come from? He'd been excited by the sudden inspiration he'd experienced at the restaurant, but it was only one of several such insights. Doctoral students had them all the time. It was part of moving forward.

Liam gave his word that all he'd done was to mention to the dean that Rupert's doctorate was progressing well, and that he'd

33

made a significant advance. And where had they managed to get the photographs? A call to his mother gave no clue. 'I'd have gladly given all of them, dear, if anyone had asked,' she said proudly.

When he entered the refectory at the university that morning, students and staff alike stood and applauded. He bowed graciously and retreated.

'Have you seen the press?' Rupert asked his dean.

'It's not just the press,' was the reply. 'I've been answering calls late last night and early this morning from all over the world, from Sweden, Canada, Turkey, Iceland, Spain. I've asked Miss Blunden to field all calls this morning. And the television channels are competing for the rights for a live telecast of your presentation to the world. The vice chancellor is insisting that it take place here at Bligh in the great hall. You'll fall over when I tell you what they're willing to pay the university. And I imagine there'll be a nice little earner for you.'

'But my discovery wasn't that stupendous,' began Rupert, feeling increasingly more threatened.

'Nonsense,' came the response. 'It'd better be, hadn't it?' the dean smiled, winked, tapped Rupert affectionately on the shoulder, and hurried away to the vice chancellor's office to negotiate television rights.

Rupert retreated from his room to escape the non-stop ringing of the phone, and the constant door knocking of well-wishers, and those anxious to declare their allegiance.

'Whatever happened?' he asked Liam, though the question was rhetorical. 'It goes from bad to worse. What am I going to do?'

The two friends sat in silence for several minutes.

'I don't suppose you have enough to report, something really meaningful to say?' Liam finally asked lamely.

Rupert merely looked at his friend and sighed. The question didn't need answering. 'There goes a promising career,' he finally said. 'I'll be a laughing stock.'

Now Liam didn't answer. There was no point disagreeing with the obvious.

'The world will be watching to hear me utter a lot of nonsense.'

A minute passed.

'That's it,' Liam suddenly brightened. 'Of course you will! You'll be speaking nonsense.'

*

The university was pleased that the Australian Broadcasting Corporation won the telecast rights over the Prime Media Group. There would be no ads or facile commentary. The dean and vice chancellor extracted a guarantee that the university would be given additional background coverage – a walk through the quadrangle focusing on the sandstone walls and gargoyles as the vice chancellor explained the history, perhaps Rupert in the library in deep conversation with some undergraduates. It would be wonderful publicity.

The township of Bligh was excited as the event approached. It had suddenly come to light on the world map. The streets were free of rubbish. Bunting appeared on shop awnings, the newsagent did a trade in memo pads with the university crest, and the cake shop sold buns shaped into Rs for Rupert. Motels were already doing a brisk trade, and real estate agents licked their lips.

'It'll be fine,' Liam assured Rupert

'You don't think it could go horribly wrong?' Rupert queried.

'Not a chance,' his friend replied confidently, and patted Rupert's shoulder, but Rupert didn't see the concerned look on his face as he walked away.

The time finally came. The great hall was packed. There'd been a ballot for seats. Lighting was tested.

A young woman applied his make-up. 'I'm having some problems with my husband,' she began, anticipating an instant solution or blessing, but he was whisked away before he could answer for final instructions from the director, was positioned on stage, and 3, 2, 1, he was live to half the world.

He launched immediately into the crux of the matter. 'It's audling, miskous audling, and the audling has to be miskous. Because we know the sablistic and the vempit, we audle, miskously.' He continued with his presentation for the next eight minutes to a dumbstruck live and television audience of millions, concluding with the reassuring 'Life is a mundle of saitches, each with patungal and klane, we know, yes we know the sablistic and vempit, and so we audle miskously.'

Five or six seconds of complete silence followed before a few people in the audience stood to their feet to applaud. The whole auditorium instantly followed suit, standing and clapping. Shouts of 'Bravo' reverberated around the hall. The cameramen worked busily, scanning enraptured and tearful faces. Everyone remained standing as Rupert departed down the centre aisle with a host of camera crew stumbling in front of him to capture a moment of history. He accepted the adulation unassumingly.

'A triumph,' a delighted Liam later told him when they finally had a moment alone. 'A real triumph.'

And it wasn't long before the plaudits arrived from the other side of the world, from Tan Sung in China, Ortega in Spain, Laxness in Iceland and Sienkiewicz in Poland.

'It goes so much further than Descartes,' one notable academic proclaimed.

'It really puts Kant's categorical imperative to the sword,' another remarked.

After a few days during which Rupert basked in the glory, academics started to do what they do best – question the veracity of propositions. 'But does the audling always have to be miskous?' Polonov from the Ukraine queried, and so a number of related debates began.

'Patungal, I accept,' said Arnaud from France, 'but I'm not so sure about klane.'

Rupert avoided discourse in these early days and remained in his office, or spent time off campus with Liam. It was too early yet to engage in debate, and he was uncertain as to how to proceed. Better to let the dust settle.

\*

As the weeks passed, Rupert was increasingly revered in the faculty, and was notified that he would be awarded honorary doctorates by three overseas universities. He was invited to lead a number of local and interstate discussions that were more presentations than seminars because there was minimal interaction. Participants didn't know what questions to ask, and Rupert felt that he was able to acquit himself well with the rare non-substantive inquiry.

He appeared on several television programs, sometimes with the ABC, where he was asked about his early life, his professional background and his future aspirations, and sometimes on reality and game shows, seemingly to further his appeal as a man of the people, and not just some ivory-tower academic.

The repercussions of his presentation had not been disastrous as he'd feared and, as his intellectual status was unique, and his charm impressive, he began to enjoy the attention he was receiving. Academics and the clergy begged for an audience, and there were emailed offers of marriage, some with modest and some with naked photographs.

His composure was tested a couple of months after the presentation when Liam showed him the evening edition of the *City Gazette*. Sandy Bucholtz, an American from a Texas university, was challenging the 'ultimate philosophy', as Rupert's theory was now called, and was gathering as yet only modest international support for his own theory. 'Life is a druk of messticles,' it began. 'It blounts the floeboe semostically.'

'How dare he!' Rupert was furious.

'Don't worry,' Liam told him, 'it was inevitable. You were successful. There'll always be someone wanting to challenge you, to knock you down or, if not, at least to jump on the bandwagon.'

Rupert could see his friend's wisdom, and decided that he hadn't been active enough in promoting his theory. And so began a lecture tour around the Australian states in a bus that Bligh purchased with money from the presentation. Rupert's face was painted on the side, with 'The Ultimate Philosophy' in bold black lettering.

The university printed spiral-bound, glossy-covered booklets of Rupert's theory with an appendix of the university's course offerings, and distributed them to universities and secondary schools in Australia and abroad.

There was occasional reporting of still more theories. But apart from the Bucholtz theory, they were short-lived, and usually discredited.

*

The months passed, and Liam was becoming increasingly uncomfortable. Rupert was dashing about the country extolling his theory in universities and schools. He'd been on two overseas trips, and he continued to be revered at home and abroad. People, particularly young women, competed for autographs and selfies with him.

'Do you think there's a danger, mate, that your head is becoming bigger than the one painted on the bus?' he asked Rupert in his usual jocular way.

'Not quite that big,' Rupert enjoyed the ribbing, and then more seriously, 'it's important that I continue with this, Liam. I owe it to all the people out there who look to me, who look to my theory for guidance, the disillusioned adolescents, the jilted lovers, the single parents trying to rear kids on a handful of dollars, the dispossessed and homeless, the middle-aged with their memories and regrets, the old men and women facing an uncertain future here and beyond...'

'I don't believe this, Rupert! How does your theory help them?' Liam was annoyed and confrontational. 'What does it do for the adolescents, the middle-aged, the homeless and the old? Does it change their lives? How does it improve the lot of mankind?' He looked intently at an indignant Rupert, and continued. 'I was with you, remember! It was my idea! You know that everything you said was absolute nonsense, deliberately so. It was mumbo jumbo.'

The atmosphere was icy now. They were silent. Liam had said his piece, and looked to Rupert for some small sign of humility.

Rupert surveyed him with a look of distaste. His fists were clenched in anger, his voice was bitter. 'I think you're jealous. It's people like you who delight in the ills of the world, people like you who stand in the way of freedom, happiness and peace of mind. A loyal friend you turned out to be!' and upturning the coffee table in a gesture of defiance, he strode away.

And so the world rolled on, a mundle of saitches in patungal and klane, and miskous audling.

# Wag

'I'm smitten,' he said. 'I know that people say love at first sight is a cliché, but how else can it be described, what other word can you use to capture the suddenness and power of such a feeling?'

A comment like this would normally be made after weeks or months of dating, and on the privacy of a couch at home with a soft music accompaniment, or at a corner table in a restaurant over an expensive meal, or in a secluded spot outside with a view of trees or ocean, and at sunrise or sunset. But not in a department store with customers in earshot, and a counter separating speaker and listener.

The speaker was twenty-seven-year-old Toby Sinclair, and the listener, Terri Armitage, who stood bewildered behind the jewellery counter of a prestige city department store. Bewildered because Toby, who she'd never met before, approached the counter empty-handed, and had launched into this declaration, if that's what it was. She didn't even have the time for the customary 'May I help you, sir?'

'Sometimes there's chemistry between two people,' Toby continued. 'I felt it instantly as soon as I laid eyes on you. Did you feel any spark?' he entreated, searching her face.

Perhaps some young women, when met with such an overture, might smile and say, 'Oh sure, yes, instant for me too,' and treat the episode as a joke. Others might choose to ignore, and utter the words that Terri didn't have a chance to say, 'May I help you, sir?' Terri's response was neither. It was more one of puzzlement, and embarrassment, and therefore silence.

Toby was a wag, someone who liked to joke, to use humour as a way of making people feel at ease. He didn't go in for the practical jokes that were often practised as initiations in fraternities, jokes that caused discomfort or humiliation like rotten-egg gas, pouring water over someone's head, or smearing something nasty over lavatory seats. He did once super glue a fifty-cent piece to the pavement and watch a woman try for five minutes to dislodge it with her walking stick, and on another occasion, when acting as MC at a wedding, he announced that one of his friends, who was tone-deaf, was to sing 'Amazing Grace', but most of his jokes were fun email messages like enquiring when one of his female friends would next be publicly dancing naked at midnight, or congratulating a male friend for a fictional feat.

Terri was at a loss to answer, so Toby continued. 'It's more than a spark for me,' he said. 'A spark is momentary, short-lived and easily extinguished. This is more like a fire.'

Two of Toby's friends stood nearby, but their faces betrayed no particular emotion.

A woman who had previously pointed out a brooch to Terri's serving companion, and still waited at the counter, followed the proceedings with a smile. 'Aren't you going to say something to the gentleman?' she said to Terri. 'My hubby has never said anything like that to me.'

Several minutes later when the woman had been served, and Toby and his friends had gone, Terri turned to her serving companion, Anna, and asked falteringly, 'What did you make of that?'

Anna was just as perplexed. 'I'm not sure,' she said and smiled. 'He wasn't grinning, and neither were his friends…and when he left, he seemed, oh, I don't know, disappointed, or at least a bit flat that you hadn't said anything.'

'What did you think of him?' Terri asked. For her, the event wasn't easy to dismiss.

'I'm jealous,' Anna replied light-heartedly. 'I think he was a bit of all right, so if you don't want the calling card he left…but more to the point…what did you think of him?'

'Yes,' Terri answered absent-mindedly, not committing herself, and said no more.

Toby had been flat, as Anna observed, and not because his avowals weren't returned. He was particularly sensitive to the needs of others, had a well developed emotional intelligence, and was concerned that he might have caused the young woman, whose name appeared on a name tag pinned to her blouse, unnecessary embarrassment. Had he gone too far? It was a joke, but had he kept on with it for too long? Once he'd committed himself to the performance, it had become difficult to stop.

Aware that jokes could often be a two-edged sword, he asked his friend Craig how he had interpreted Terri's reaction, received a vague answer, and wondered if he should return to the shop the next day and apologise. That would be excruciating, and after all, it should have been obvious that it had all been in good fun.

*

The next day, Toby received an email that read,

Dear Toby,

I'm the girl that you spoke to yesterday at the shop and my name is Terri Armitage. You said that you often know instantly how you feel, and you asked me if there was any spark for me. I want to thank you for being so honest with me. None of the men I've known have ever been that open with me before, and don't seem to be good at expressing their real feelings. I'm really sorry that you went away without any answer from me. Please forgive me, but it all came as a bit of a shock and surprise for me.

I wonder if strong feeling or love isn't immediate for some of us, but rather creeps up. You asked me, and I want you to know that the answer is yes. There was a spark, and since yesterday, I have thought a lot about what you said, and my feelings have got stronger. I wonder if what we think and what we feel go together?

Anyway, I do feel like you, and would like to see you again, and preferably not across a counter.

Yours sincerely,

Terri.

*

'What am I going to do?' a disconcerted Toby asked his friend Craig.

'What do you feel like doing?' Craig replied. 'If you like her, then go ahead, ask her out. The way is clear. If you don't want to, tell her it was a joke, or at least a misunderstanding.'

'She seemed nice enough,' Toby spoke as much to himself as to his friend. 'But I don't know her. I have the sense that we don't share much in common at all. I don't feel anything much.'

Craig shrugged as if the solution was clear. What was the problem? But Toby was anxious. He had been misleading, and he didn't want any suffering on his account.

His reply email was short and to the point:

Hi Terri,

If you're free after work tomorrow, we could meet at Harrison's, say 5.15 p.m. Let me know if it doesn't suit.

Toby.

\*

The meeting started awkwardly. She rushed into the restaurant looking elegant in a tight black skirt, high heels and cream Edwardian blouse. She'd obviously gone to a lot of trouble dressing and grooming for the occasion. He was wearing jeans, and had to remove his hands from his pockets to return her embrace.

She held him at arm's length for several seconds, looking affectionately into his eyes before sitting down. 'At last,' she said. 'It's so good to see you again.'

It seemed that it was her turn to be assured, and his to be bewildered.

They ordered and chatted, though most of the talk was hers.

'About the other day,' Toby began on a couple of occasions with the intention, not of dismissing everything he'd said as a joke, but of putting it in a better, perhaps a more light-hearted perspective, but each time Terri made use of his awkward pause.

'I feel so lucky,' she said. 'Anna reckoned it was so romantic, and while I was taken by surprise, I can see now that it was.'

43

And that was sufficient to weaken Toby's resolve. So most of the time they spent sharing the details of their lives.

'I want to know everything about you,' Terri said, and took his hand across the table. 'I want to know what makes you tick.'

And when the feelings of yesterday weren't mentioned, Toby felt on safer ground.

When they left, she kissed him on the cheek, secured his mobile number, and told him tenderly that she returned his declared feeling of the day before, plus interest.

Her email that night read,

Darling Toby,

Had a wonderful time. It was so nice to see you, hear about your life, and even to touch you. Looking forward to more! It's the most binding thing when two people share with each other, isn't it? Tomorrow?

Love, Terri xx

*

'I'm in deep now,' Toby told Craig. 'She's nice, but not my type. I've tried to tell her, but whenever I do, she talks about how great it all is, how she's been waiting for this moment all her life, and I lose my nerve.'

Craig, one of the great exponents of clichés, could only contribute 'Sometimes you have to be cruel to be kind.'

The next day's email reported that she had told her parents about him, and that they were looking forward to meeting him. It concluded with at least thirty kisses.

*

'Do you still feel as strongly as you did that first day?' Terri asked him.

It was the fourth day of their whirlwind relationship, and they were sitting in the same restaurant they'd occupied for the three previous days.

44

Craig was there too because Terri was anxious to meet his friends. As yet, there had been no opportunity for more intimate sharing.

Toby shifted uneasily in his seat, and attempted to evade the question without being hurtful, and he didn't want to carry on a conversation like this with Craig present. 'I think you're a very impressive person,' he replied, and a few moments of silence followed.

'You know what, Toby,' she said, with a sudden hardness and lack of warmth, 'you might be a nice person too, but all I can see is someone who waltzed into my work, and took delight in embarrassing me in front of my colleagues. Do you really think I give a hoot about you? Well, I don't! Do you realise how hard it was for me to keep up the charade, all those lovey-dovey emails, all that pretence? Now the joke's on you,' and she stood up, emptied the remaining half glass of her white wine over his head, and walked out.

There were smiles and tittering from the restaurant crowd thirsty for others' misadventure.

If Toby felt chastened and embarrassed, Craig felt indignant. 'How dare she,' he stormed as they made their way home. 'But that, my friend, is what you get for trying to be nice to her. You should have told her when you had the chance. Anyway, it should be a relief. It's solved your problem.'

*

For several of the following days, Toby was depressed, not because of the scene she had orchestrated, and the embarrassment it caused, but because he had hurt someone sufficiently to have made them retaliate in that way. He considered emailing to apologise but didn't do so. No more joking, he told himself. Never again. It's the perfect example of how something can be misinterpreted. And some people find it hard to read irony anyway.

A week later, his depression had deepened, and Craig had tried a couple of times to get him out of the house.

'You know, mate,' Toby told his friend, 'the joke is well and truly on me.'

'You're taking it too hard, aren't you?' Craig answered. 'All right, she might have been embarrassed, but what she did to you was a lot worse.'

'No, it's not that,' Toby replied. 'I miss her,' he said softly.

Craig was amazed. 'You don't mean to say you've fallen for her?'

Toby nodded. 'Don't ask me why. I can't figure it,' he continued. 'Can anyone ever figure why?'

'But you said you don't have anything in common,' Craig offered as evidence. 'Are you sure this isn't some misguided, or rather distorted, sympathy, some need to be penitent?'

'It's not sympathy, and of course we don't have much in common,' Toby answered. 'That was obvious the first time in the restaurant when we talked. But there was so much I saw of her strength, and her caring, her resilience, so much I admired. I know the differences would have continued to exist, but we might have been very happy if we could have succeeded in loving the differences between us. Isn't that what love is about?'

Craig didn't have an opinion. He knew that love was finding perfection in another, and he didn't share Toby's view of Terri's perfection. 'Well, you'll know better next time,' he said, and believing that love involved submission to the loved one, knew there was no point encouraging Toby to take the matter further. 'But you can't go on moping about the place. It's time to move on.'

*

Terri was subdued after the restaurant episode. She felt a little ashamed because it was so unlike her. She wasn't what her parents had deprecatingly called a women's libber. She wasn't aggressive, or even assertive. She prided herself on her old-fashioned ladylike qualities. It had never been her intention to make such a scene. She wanted

Craig there so that Toby could be embarrassed in the way she had been in front of Anna. But she had never intended to empty her wine over his head. It was a sudden impulse fired by an emotion charged situation. She could still see Toby, open-mouthed, head bowed with hair dripping as she walked out. She could hear the restaurant laughter, imagine the smiles. No, it wasn't like her at all.

'Good for you.' Anna was delighted with her friend's gesture.

'No, Anna,' Terri responded, 'it was cruel…and I don't think he ever intended to hurt me. He was just acting the goat.'

'You're not feeling sorry for him, are you?' a surprised Anna asked.

Terri didn't answer. She just continued to look glum.

'I don't believe it,' Anna continued. 'I don't believe it. You really care for him, don't you?'

Again there was no answer, but that was sufficient confirmation.

'What'll I do, Anna?' Terri asked tearfully. 'He certainly won't want to hear from me again. He'll probably hate me.'

The two friends were busy serving customers for the rest of the day, and there was no time to talk further until the shop closed.

'The way forward is clear,' Anna, having had time to think about it all, resumed as they left. 'After what you've done, the ball is in your court. If you feel that sorry, then tell him, and if you can't tell him how you really feel, at least ask him out for a coffee…as an apology…then see what happens.'

The email Toby received that night read,

Dear Toby,

I'm not joking now. You really must believe that. I'm deadly serious. What I did at the restaurant was terrible and I'm really sorry. I'm ashamed of myself. You have no reason to believe this, after how I've behaved, but I really do care for you. No, it's more than care. I don't want to say it in an email. It seems too formal or something. If you don't hate me, I'd like to see you again. I'll wait to hear from you, and if you don't want to see me, at least forgive me.

Terri.

\*

Terri was on tenter-hooks for two days, convinced that she would hear nothing. She was miserable and had to be consoled by Anna.

The small parcel arrived at work in a break between serving customers. The gold-beribboned box certainly wasn't stock for the store, for her name was clearly printed on a label. Unfastening the clasp, she saw a very expensive emerald bracelet alight with green fire on black velvet. Serving at a jewellery counter, she had a good idea of the cost of such a gift. She was overwhelmed. And there was an unsigned note inside that read, 'Thought you might have some use for this – found it on the council tip – looking forward to another alcoholic shower tonight.'

# Pursuit

Why about me? Because to some degree it's what Julian Freud said about everything we write being an autobiography. But also because I've been told by well-meaning friends that the writer is unusually and even bizarrely atypical, not the normal new-age, or for that matter old-age, man. So the events should not be left to speak entirely for themselves. While they may reveal certain truths, while their occurrence is irrefutable, while unfortunately there are too many witnesses to attempt denial, a credible understanding needs further light shed on the protagonist.

Already you're suspicious, particularly those of you who believe that actions speak louder than words. Surely it's possible that sometimes actions belie intention. Between the idea and the reality falls the shadow. He's attempting to justify himself before he's even started, you're thinking to yourself. It may seem a lame defence to you, but surely there is a difference between explanation and justification.

The nature-nurture argument is a cliché, and a red herring. Who can tell? Serial offenders emerge from loving and supportive homes. Gentle souls are the product of harsh backgrounds. Parents and their offspring are chalk and cheese. I don't know what, if anything, I've inherited to make me the way I am. Perhaps I was simply infused with more than my fair share of oestrogen.

It's said that romantic love is the product of sex restrictions. We idealise imagined realities. And what more seductive realities are there to imagine than love, and sex? That's nurture, but at least we're on surer ground. On my fourteenth birthday, my father's only agency of sex education, and confirmation that sex was something that needed restricting, was a book, proffered charily before his quick retreat and

49

out-the-door unfinished 'If there's anything…' leaving me mulling over diagrams of all our reproductive bits that produced a burgeoning disquiet of how my wriggly bits assaulted eggs, and evoked thoughts of the chook house beneath the mulberry tree.

At school, a single-sex high school of caged males with seething hormones, sex was regarded as something boys inflicted on hapless girls, and celebrated with ribaldry and talk of hyperbolic body parts, and sometimes with shocked envy, 'Billy's done it,' as the boys all nursed sodden, privately unsatisfied desire.

My church youth group, the nucleus of my social life as a teenager, was didactic but too unsure of itself to be sanctimonious. The church itself conceded sex a rightful place but, beyond the sanctioned limits, it was a sin, a word that trembled with its fire and brimstone penalties and biblical injunctions lathered from the pulpit. It was not even something you could approach by stealth or edge enjoyably towards because the devil triumphed over paltry human will. The canon's sermon of 'first you leave, then you cleave' still resonates, and I smile when I think of how modern youth would enjoy their parody of cleaving with some of its more earthy equivalents.

Of course these were the days history and culture colluded to create a very different world. It was a time before the advent of the internet and social media, and therefore a time before individuality, even idiosyncrasy, was heralded as normal, and we were left to feel unvintaged, and suffer the perils of feeling unique, quite unlike anyone else. It was a time before the stricken male-only overtures of asking a girl for a date were replaced by the unashamed swapping of mind and body credentials on the internet, often with the same uninhibited and reciprocated desire for genital greetings.

Little wonder then that something in the nature-nurture mix made me what I am. To call myself a romantic is a bit glib. But if it means someone who believes in ideal love and sentiment, I suppose I am. In my adolescent years, I'd look out from the cocoon of my tiny bedroom, across the night sky pierced to weeping by the stars, and dream of what most of us have at some time or other dreamt. Is there someone out there for me?

Girls were special. They didn't have the bravado and hubris of boys. They were warm and sensitive. I found that appealing. I'm not sure where my chivalry came from. Stories of knights, of champions deferring to their ladies fair. Reading of courtly conventions. Perhaps some delicate balance of nature and nurture. Well into my middle age, and at a time of relative sexual equality, and even a time when some women regarded male deference as insulting, I'd stand in trains and buses for women half my age. Some looked a little bewildered. A few passengers smirked. Most were indifferent. But at least an occasional one affirmed by a word or nod that my gallant world hadn't entirely passed me by.

That's enough. I think you get the picture.

*

Her name's not important. Names often position a person in the reader's mind. If it's a name we like, one that has exotic appeal, or that belongs to someone special in our life, we are favourably predisposed. If it's the name of the feared harridan aunt of our childhood, then the romance I'm trying to conjure is threatened. So I'll simply refer to her as 'she'. And I'll avoid the amorous sobriquets of petal, heart of my heart, snookums and even darling.

I've always thought that readers tend to scan quickly over a physical description of a character, rather than try to form an exact mental picture, so I'll confine myself to a few broad brushstrokes, and hope my infatuation doesn't colour things too much. When I first met her, I was instantly besotted. She had pale gold hair like a picture-book fairy princess, unusual cornflower-blue eyes, and a full and shapely figure. Her assurance was such that she seemed to glide rather than walk.

Fate, that usually plays tricks and laughs at us, was kind for once, for having introduced us, our hostess left to welcome others, and we found ourselves alone. I feel she was captivated too, because as we talked, she kept shifting feet and averting her eyes to look at others across the room, a sure sign that she was finding it difficult to cope with the intensity of her emotion. Occasionally she'd sigh. I don't remember what self-deprecating comment she uttered, but I do recall my unwillingness to accept her self-criticisms, whether they were genuine or feigned self-praise. And I told her so.

'Don't put me on a pedestal,' she said indifferently. I can still hear the timbre of her voice. 'Don't put me on a pedestal.' And that's when it all began.

'Pedestal': 'a position of eminence or supposed superiority'. That's just what I will do, I decided. I'll put her on a pedestal, so others can share my infatuation. But they won't share her gratitude for being so feted.

At considerable expense, I ordered a seventy-five-centimetre-square block of pure white Carrara marble that she could stand on and be observed by an adoring public. Before its arrival, I entertained visions of her standing demurely on my pedestal, perhaps with a slight air of disinterest, dressed in a flowing white robe like a Greek goddess, while people gathered to cheer, or watch in silent awe.

But I hadn't thought my venture through properly, for when the delivery finally came, and I saw the small crane lifting the marble block from the back of the truck, I knew my cause was lost. And I couldn't invite all and sundry into my house to behold her, because the block, once positioned, fell through the floor with a resounding splintering of floorboards, and toppled sideways so that only a long sharp edge protruded a few centimetres from the gaping hole. At least she wasn't privy to that faux pas.

So, abandoning the idea of a marble base, I decided on something portable, something I could tow with the car, and something she could mount with haste when I took her on harbour walks or visits to a park or city square. I could watch the crowds stare in admiration, indulge the odd aside, perhaps with a nonchalant air, and bathe in lover's pride. I'd build a podium on wheels.

Not having much experience as a builder, I enlisted the help of my mate Gavin. We purchased a very old and long-disused trailer, and proceeded to erect a wooden platform atop that she could mount on steps, and peer at an enthusiastic crowd from a great height. She would be raised to the Gods and be there for all to see. It was a labour of love.

Gavin arranged for his electrician friend to drape the structure with various coloured lights that could be operated from the car to flash intermittently, and signal the event. But the real tour de force was my finding two matching, near-antique brass horns, the ones they used to have on the very first automobiles, that you operate by squeezing an inflated rubber pouch. These were secured to each side of our wooden structure. It took a couple of weeks, but we eventually had the pleasure of standing back and admiring our work.

'This will sweep her off her feet, mate,' Gavin said.

And I shared his optimism.

On our first trial run, we were stopped by two policemen who wanted to know, 'What the hell is this?'

'You're telling me,' the burly one said after I'd explained, 'you're going to drive this around and about so that some woman or goddess or something can climb up there and show herself?'

'Do they mean naked, chief?' the junior officer added with febrile interest.

'She won't be naked,' Gavin answered for me, 'but yes, that's about the strength of it.'

The two policemen moved a little way off to confer, both looking back every few seconds with incredulity, while Gavin tested the flashing lights and honked the horns.

'We could take you to the station,' the burly one said uncertainly, 'but we'll settle for the Department of Main Roads.'

After several departmental officers inspected our invention, some shaking their heads, others grinning, it was designated a 'Class 2 Short-Towing Vehicle', in brackets 'Podium', and we were warned against flashing lights and honking while in transit.

We were ready. The day had finally arrived, and I had managed to keep our labours on her behalf a secret. It was a public holiday, and the parks would be full of people. Full of admirers.

'You can't be serious,' she responded in disbelief as I explained the purpose of our trip.

I was delighted. She was obviously overcome with emotion. Perhaps her reluctance was a case of reality falling short of long-cherished expectation. It took some time to convince her, but finally she agreed to at least come for the ride.

It was a bright blue morning when we left in the Holden, towing the podium. It's difficult to convey in words my excited anticipation, and the pleasure of fulfilling another's dreams. Gavin waved goodbye, and she sat beside me staring ahead in silence.

The eleven o'clock news reported two northbound lanes closed on the M1, and traffic banked up for fourteen kilometres. The live telecast showed an empty trailer and a mass of splintered wood, streamers and electrical cord strewn across the road. Some red and blue lights winked feebly and died. A blonde-haired, blue-eyed woman was standing outside the car shrieking, and waving her finger at a man who sat motionless inside. A stony-faced policeman walked towards the car but jumped in alarm for all the world to see, having trodden on the rubber squeezy of a horn that protested loudly.

I didn't blame her for being annoyed. When you look forward to something so much, and it's denied you, it must hurt. The reassurances of love, and my undying commitment did little to soothe, and it was several weeks before our next strained conversation.

My resolve was weakened, but I was still determined that others should share my adoration. So as a last resort I found an old wooden fruit box in the tool shed that she could stand on, tore off the label for Goulburn Valley pears, and coaxed her to stand on its end.

'A rehearsal,' I explained. 'I could paint the box, or just cover it in coloured crepe paper.'

Reluctantly, she hoisted herself up on one foot, but when she planted both feet on the box, she fell straight through the rotten thing, screaming obscenities. Her pantyhose was shredded and her shins were bleeding. Her legs were pinioned by broken wooden slats, and I had to gently pry them loose to free her.

Of course I was devastated. This was clearly my fault, but perhaps in time she'd realise that my motives had been worthy. I simply wanted her to enjoy the worship from others that I felt, to put her on the pedestal she didn't think she deserved.

'Next time, mate,' Gavin chuckled, 'you'll buy a trenching tool and put her in a hole.'

*

Freud had a term for it. Reaction formation. People display the opposite emotion to the one they're really feeling. It's a defence mechanism. So she didn't fool me. After nearly a month, her apparent indifference and residual hostility disguised her real feelings.

While pondering this, it occurred to me that in my desperation to exalt her, I had failed to reveal anything of myself. So how was I to go about it? There are two dichotomous schools of thought: one that girls like men to be tough, to display their masculinity, and the other that they like to see a man's vulnerability. I decided on the former. There was time enough for the latter. If she could witness the scope of my physical talents and courage, it would surely melt all resistance. And so I pleaded with her to come with me to the city's recreation park.

She was decidedly cool after our previous escapades, but finally relented. 'You promise me I won't have to do anything,' she demanded, 'no public viewing, and I can go to any stall, on any ride I like.'

Of course I promised. I only wanted her to watch me.

It was a glorious day. Families were sprawled on the lawns. Small children soaked their faces in melting Neapolitan ice cream, or bawled when a double scoop inevitably dropped to the pavement, and adolescents imbibed acne through cans of Coca Cola and kissed furtively. She won a kewpie doll on a stick from knocking over skittles, and a small cuddly toy from dropping balls in the mouths of clowns. Things were certainly looking up.

Strolling together through the park, we passed a boxing tent where a spruiker with a hand-held microphone was calling for men to challenge one of his fighters. Two of them stood oil-shiny and bare-chested on the stage in satin shorts, pounding their boxing gloves together as if to advertise their power. Other fighters had enticed opponents already, and waited inside the tent as the audience filed in, seduced by the taunts of the alliteratively named boxers that 'I'll punch his head in'.

I know she looked at me. Perhaps it was only to suss out my reaction to this strange expression of masculine culture. Or did that look carry another expectation? Whichever, I seized the opportunity, and climbed onto the stage, braving the 'no kidding' face of the nearest boxer.

No, I'd never boxed, and no, I'd never been in a scrap before, but this was something I had to do. I was to fight in the first bout, so I was spared the nervousness of waiting. I was given an ill-fitting pair of shorts and a dirty singlet that two of me could climb into. And the clang of the bell was jarring.

I woke up in a back section of the tent, curtained off from the crowd. For a while, it was difficult to focus through swollen eyes, but I was able to make out my two front teeth loosely wrapped in a tissue and sitting on my chest. When we resumed our walk through the park, she was silent, neither critical nor solicitous. She didn't ask how I felt. So I knew I still had something to prove.

'Look at that,' she said admiringly, taking my arm, and we watched a man plunge feet first from a platform at least eighty metres above a shallow lake, secured by an elastic cable that extended with the weight of his jump to leave him dangling a couple of metres above the water before the elastic retracted to propel him upwards.

'It's called bunji jumping,' I told her.

'Well, you wouldn't get me doing it,' she said with a shudder.

I suppose a challenge can take many forms. It can be explicit by spelling out exactly what a person has to do. It can be vicarious by asking a person how they'd feel about doing it. Or it might even be suggestive or evocative. Her comment was the latter. Merely by suggesting the courage needed, the challenge had been issued.

And so I climbed the countless steps to a small platform and, without wishing to boast, I felt no fear. I could see her well below, very small but discernible among a melange of colour, craning her neck to look up. At last, I had a captive audience. At least it was an audience of one. I would make this spectacular. No timid stepping off the platform with a vertical right-way-up drop. That was too easy. This would be the affirmation of my love.

I know it's a cliché but I felt my heart burst forth in song as I jumped, throwing myself forward into a swallow dive, horizontal for a moment with my arms spread out gracefully like wings, before I dropped. For a fraction of a second, I thought the shouting behind me was acclamation until I realised my harness wasn't on.

They dug my head out from the silt of the lake, for I was buried deep, half submerged, fixed vertically upside-down, I was later told, with my white feet extruding. I won't bore you with details of my rescue, the seriousness of which degenerated into hilarity for the crowd, or my long recuperation, but I was later told by Gavin that my exploits had become a household joke, and that people rolled off their chairs at dinner to screech and choke with mirth as they recounted the episode.

For some months, I was plastered neck to knee, and was cruelly disappointed she didn't visit me in hospital, until I learned that she had also had a short stint there, having tumbled while entertaining friends.

*

Don't underestimate family. It's where we learn how to think and act and simply be. If there's any merit in the claim that most of what we are, or will become, is ingrained by the time we're five, the significance of family is obvious. Even in those families where a child feels an antipathy towards a parent, the need for affirmation remains strong – the desire to confirm that a life has not been a betrayal. How often do we return to where we grew up to reclaim our roots, or to rediscover who we are, or how we've evolved?

To reclaim her heart, I realised that I would need her parents' support, or at least their acceptance. Of course I wanted to like them, and for them to like me, because they were a large part of her life, even though she'd rarely spoken of them. But there was more strategy in my reckoning. I was presenting as one who valued the most fundamental of human institutions.

My hints about getting an invitation to her home for dinner to meet her parents fell on deaf ears. She still blamed me for falling off her chair and spraining her wrist, though I never understood why, and she never missed an opportunity to point to the faint scars on her legs. So I had to virtually invite myself.

'Why,' she expostulated, 'haven't you got anything to eat at your own home?' But eventually she relented and a date was grudgingly set.

I donned my best clothes, tailored charcoal trousers and a blue cashmere sweater, and met her at the door. She seemed uneasy as she formally introduced her parents, but didn't take my hand, or intimate anything special in our relationship. Her mother was a plumper and more wrinkled version of herself, and circumspect to the point of being prim. The house was spotless, and everything had its place, angled for the best advantage. Almost curtseying as she left for the kitchen, I found myself bowing ever so slightly.

Her father was tall and nondescript, probably henpecked, but we managed some broken and uncomfortable conversation until he mentioned his passion for golf. 'I'm off 27 now,' he enthused, speaking of his handicap, and thankfully coming alive.

I'd been waiting for an opening, and this was it. I'd played golf the previous weekend, and was still glowing from my success. There was one shot in particular, a three wood green approach from two hundred metres that skidded onto the green. I'd made par. Sharing his passion now, feeling that I might have found an ally of sorts, I took a billiard cue from its rack to demonstrate, providing commentary as I did so, but my backward swing produced a deafening crash.

The glass-fronted china cabinet teetered for a couple of seconds as if in indecision, and fell. Glass exploded in knife-like shards and flew like shrapnel. China fell and met the same fate as crockery plates at a Greek wedding. Her mother, an apoplectic blue, dashed into the room and knelt, caressing broken pieces of Willow dinner service, shattered vases of Waterford crystal, Royal Dalton cups and saucers, and headless Lladro figurines.

'I'm so sorry,' I murmured. 'I'm really sorry,' I repeated. 'I didn't mean...' I began, but of course I didn't mean to do it.

As her father stood stock-still, aghast, I knelt beside her mother to rescue some of the more retrievable fragments, starting with the Venetian glasses.

'Perhaps we can...' and I left the rest unsaid. 'Do you have some superglue?'

Her mother, reduced to a state of complete helplessness and dependency, fetched the glue and I began the repair work. Her father retreated to another room. Her mother stared fixedly ahead and rocked autistically in a lounge chair. The dinner spoiled in the oven.

'Look,' I said after a couple of hours, trying to feign some enthusiasm, 'you can hardly tell these glasses have been broken.'

And feeling proud of what in the circumstances was a very modest achievement, I grasped the cup to show her mother, but it wouldn't come. It – and, as I soon found, every other cup I'd repaired – was stuck. I'd used the dining room table to glue the cups and they were stuck to it. I imagined every future dinner guest in need of a drink having to stoop and suck.

It was time to go. I'd certainly outworn my welcome. I was ushered to a side door, presumably because splinters of glass littered the way to the front entrance, or so I would avoid the Rodinesque brass on an antique Sunderland table in the foyer, but tradesman had left a large can of paint they'd been using against the door-frame. It really isn't my fault, I told myself as four litres of Taubman's canary yellow super gloss gobbled carpet pile and ran molten through the hall. Her father was nowhere to be seen. Mother sat in the same lounge chair, catatonic.

It's said that every cloud has a silver lining, which is really an empty statement based on probabilities. It's not so much that good actually comes from bad, but that life is full of both, and the law of averages demands that each will have its turn. But there was some good, and never in the way anyone could have predicted. She came to me the following day, ostensibly with wounded pride, but she couldn't maintain the pretence, and was more affectionate than she'd ever been, claiming that her parents watched over her every movement, and told her what she should feel and think, and how she should act.

'It was good to see us,' note the use of the plural, 'get one back.'

*

'It is a truth universally acknowledged that a single man blah blah must be in want of a wife.' *Pride and Prejudice* of course, though this man was not in possession of a good fortune. I'd loved, I'd worshipped her ever since we'd first met, and I always wanted to be with her, but marriage hadn't entered the equation. It had now. It might have been the pleasure of her snuggling up with me, a rare expression of emotion, or that feeling of something peaceful, something settling in her parent's home.

I'd worked hard at impressing. Perhaps it was time for commitment. Surely a willingness to commit was the most impressive thing of all. I was surprised I hadn't thought of it earlier. This conviction afforded me a new lease on life.

I did the rounds of the local shops, and travelled to the city looking at rings, finding my search bewildering. Of course the ring had to be a little superior to what I could glean from the packet of cornflakes, but the price tags of thousands of dollars were beyond my comprehension for a tiny piece of glass that I could have rescued from her mother's shattered Waterford crystal. But after all the questions about the size of her fingers that I couldn't answer, and after examining the fingers of a dozen shop attendants, I eventually found a ring that I thought would suffice.

So where could I ask the question? I mulled over the possibilities: a restaurant with an expensive dinner, though as a timid soul I might be embarrassed by her reaction; the safety of my place or her home, though hers was still being restored; or a park on an idyllic day with nature as the backdrop, and in which inhibition could literally be thrown to the wind. Of course I chose the latter.

The very next day came on order. Hot and blue. For her, it was probably like any other. She looked magnificent in a soft pink cotton blouse and white slacks that covered the fading scars on her legs. The sun sparkled on the nearby lake. There were even magpies trilling. I chose my time carefully, waiting for the moment she had finished her bun, and had wiped the sugary cream from her mouth. She looked startled as I went down on bended knee.

'Is it that cramp again?' she asked dismissively.

But as she hadn't turned away, I launched into my spiel of what she meant to me, avoiding the words that would cause lisping because I still didn't have my front teeth. And with a certain flourish, I reached into my pocket and handed her a Mars bar wrap. I'd left the damned ring at home!

I don't think she'd understood the significance of the event. I suppose she was used to my foibles by then. So I tried a second time, making sure that I hadn't forgotten the ring. It was at my place, for there'd been a week of wet weather, and the park wasn't an option. I'd had the foresight to rehearse a different spiel, but as I went down on bended knee, I knelt on several drawing pins I'd dropped from a mapping exercise, and leapt several feet in the air with a mighty bellow. She must have thought I was deeply disturbed, because even though I pointed out the pins that fastened my trousers to my now bleeding knee, she left shortly afterwards.

The third attempt was also a failure. My knee was a toxic blue, and as I embarked on my new spiel, I really did experience cramp, and rolled over on my back to stretch my foot, pulling it with both hands. I continued briefly with my appeal, lying on my back, but there was no eye contact, the words came in pained gasps, and it seemed an inappropriate way to put such a momentous question. So I stopped altogether.

There was a need for time out to take stock. I let another week pass, and as I was rehearsing my fourth spiel, I decided on a different approach. I'd been kneeling. Why? Why kneel before her? I suppose grovelling is too strong a word, but it did smack of inequality. Weren't we to come together as equals, as man and wife?

And so, newly assured, I chose my time and place. I would bring her back here after dinner at the club. It would be in the lounge room. I would stand instead of kneel. So before I left on that special day, I vacuumed the floor, removed any obstacles from arms' and legs' reach, did some stretching exercises for calf and thigh muscles, and ensured that the ring was safe in my coat pocket.

I was animated returning home. Dinner had been a success, and she seemed to be more comfortable with me. Or at least less uncomfortable. This would surely be the moment we'd both recall in years to come, sitting together on the porch, holding hands, chewing over the history of our lost youth.

I wasn't going to waste any time. I sat her on the lounge and, rather than kneel, I stood on a kitchen chair that I pulled across in front of her. She looked up at me quite incredulous as I began my thrice-aborted vows with grand romantic flare. I was really outdoing myself, and I felt she was impressed, at least if her half-open mouth was any indication.

I was so overcome with emotion that I began to feel giddy with excitement. The room seemed to be spinning, slowly at first, but then with gathering pace. In a few seconds, my love became a coloured blur and I couldn't see her face. At least for a few seconds I'd experienced momentous pride, I'd felt much more a man, until my neck chain wrapped around the ceiling fan.

*

Sometimes it's important to walk away. I don't mean forever. Situations can become so intense, so fraught, that it helps to find a quiet space for a while and mentally take stock. We can often come back with a new perspective, buoyed, and find that the difficulties we once experienced have evaporated.

There'd be another proposal, hopefully only one. My commitment to marriage was entrenched. But for a while I'd decided to continue as we had been doing before, to let things simmer down. A hiatus. I'd be attentive, caring, loving, and I'd know when the time was right.

In the days that followed, I began to realise that I had been trying too hard. I'd tried to create a context in which she'd receive the public reverence and adulation she deserved. I'd tried to prove my commitment by demonstrating my physical prowess and willingness to be her champion. And I'd tried to impress her by ingratiating with her parents. Pedestals, fancy dinners, attempted feats, what were they in the scheme of things? Love isn't contingent on what we do. It resides with who we are.

So allowing time for the family to recover from my destruction of their home, I went to see her with no gifts, and no other motive beyond the simple pleasure of her company. I approached with a feeling of great relief, as if a burden had been lifted from my shoulders. But in negotiating entry to their home by the rusted metal gate, my trousers were ripped apart, and I met her antagonistic parents at the door with my backside in full view.

I hurried inside to hide my shame, pronounced in Calvin Kleins. I was a little disoriented, and feeling tenderness for her from her loyalty and magnanimity in not blaming me for so many of the last year's happenings, the painful history of our relationship, I rushed towards her for a welcoming kiss. But I didn't tilt my head, and the impact broke her nose.

It ended in a courthouse cell where I had ample time to think and ponder the happenings of the last year. I had to record these events because reality becomes distorted with each successive revisiting. Some happenings recede into the haze of our consciousness, while others, previously insignificant, loom large. It was some time ago now, so perhaps this is just a refraction of what really occurred. I think of Hamlet's claim that 'thinking makes it so'. But one thing I can say with certainty is that I was charged with obscenity and GBH. What's more, I lost the girl.

# Penelope

Well, I suppose he has a reputation for self-restraint, my Ulysses. They say that's what makes him such a good negotiator and diplomat, along with his friend Nestor. How many times over all those years did I wish he had a little less restraint, and perhaps some of Achilles' all-consuming anger? I don't mean just anger and nothing else. I mean strong emotion, passion if you like. It might have been more urgent for him then to get back home. Or he could have used his much-vaunted skills in negotiating.

Look, I know he didn't really want to go off and fight in the Trojan War. I'll give him credit for that. It wasn't like him to pretend to be mad to get out of going, just because some oracle had prophesied a long delayed return home. Unfortunately his little ruse was discovered and he had to go, but you've got to hand it to that oracle! So off he went, and Telemachus was only a babe in arms. He'd barely been named.

I know he had to go. Ten years it turned out to be. We had no idea. Yes, ten years the war lasted, but of course Ulysses didn't come home after that, did he? It was twenty years! And for all that time, I'm left to provide for myself, and to rear Telemachus alone, to serve him his soups and his flatbreads mixed with cheese or honey, and to keep him with me in the back of the house where the girls belong, rather than him being able to spend time with his father getting an education, or learning how to fight. And I can tell you, there was nothing delicate about his manners as a young boy, and trying to teach him to eat properly with his fingers. It is the Mycenaean civilisation after all! And what of Argos? He needed his bones and walks. The slaves helped but they couldn't do it all.

Others came back, though it was mainly the wounded. Ulysses

was wounded by Socus, but perhaps it wasn't serious enough to return. Anyway, they told me all the stories of how great my husband was. Ingenious, they said. He built some great horse that the Trojans found outside their gates and wheeled into Troy, and once inside, under cover of darkness, all the Greek army jumped out of its insides and wham, they surprised the Trojans and won the war. Ingenious.

Perhaps he could have shown some of that resourcefulness to get back home and help with the garden, to discipline his teenage son, and to walk the dog that fretted for him.

But that wasn't the worst of it. It was the suitors who came after the war had ended. I hated them. But then again, how could you blame them when they thought Ulysses was dead. We all did.

'You'll be the queen of my palace. You'll want for nothing,' and, 'I may not be the most influential of Greek champions, I know I'll never replace your husband in your heart, but I've done well, I'm a man of integrity, and I'll be a loyal husband,' and, 'I'm not a wealthy man, but what I lack in material possessions, I can make up for in the power of my love for you.' Give it a rest! Sound familiar? Will I go on? Most of us women have heard it all before.

I grew to hate their wheedling. I tried hiding when they called, feigned headaches. A woman must at all times be gracious with a man. Men are our masters after all. I can't help but blame Ulysses for what I had to go through. He must have known I'd be pursued by men after all that time.

As the years passed, the pressure was enormous. It doesn't seem to be acceptable for a woman not to be married, as if we should be desperate, and so I gave them an undertaking. I was weaving a burial shroud for poor old Laertes, Ulysses' dad. When it's finished, I told them, I'll choose a suitor and marry. Remember, by that stage we all assumed Ulysses was dead.

So I'd do a few hours of weaving each day, nearly going blind, and every night in those last three years I'd undo what I'd done in the day. It's just as well Laertes didn't die in the meantime! Three years, until my little deception was discovered. Only recently, though, thanks to the Gods.

Here in Ithaca they all see me as a model of virtue, and my relationship with Ulysses as one of connubial bliss. Ulysses and Penelope. I can just hear them all saying it. Ulysses and Penelope. Perhaps if one of those suitors was even a little bit attractive, it may have been a different story. Men really 'have themselves on', don't they? Anyway, those suitors paid a heavy price later for their attentions. So it's just as well there wasn't someone decent among them.

But what really upset me were all the games he had to play when he did come back. It'd been twenty years, remember. Now wouldn't you think your average man would come to the door, beside himself with joy and anticipation, even shout from the courtyard, announce himself if he's not instantly recognised, and say, 'Darling it's me, it's your Ulysses,' and take you in his arms, whisper endearments, and after bathing, and a light meal of barley bread with olives and figs prepared by Eurycleia, perhaps after giving you gifts of jewels captured from slaughtering the Trojans in Troy, lead you gently to the wedding chamber? But ah no, not Ulysses, the mighty Ulysses who returned to reassert his rightful place as King of Ithaca. He didn't say a thing!

Yes, I know, I played a game too. You see, I knew it was him all along. But he thought I hadn't recognised him when I first saw him. Eurycleia discovered his secret, and also told me, even though he'd threatened her life if she told anyone. Aren't men fools? It was a mark on one of his feet that he'd had as a boy, and she saw it when washing them.

So what could I do, I asked myself. What could I do that would make him reveal himself? Then it dawned. I would devise a contest for the suitors. The winner would get me. If there was a winner, that is! There was always the danger that Ulysses wouldn't compete in the contest I organised. There was a chance that he didn't want to return to me, in which case I might have to settle for one of my suitors some time in the future.

But I knew he couldn't resist pitting his strength and skill against other men, and I decided to make the contest so hard that Ulysses would have to win. Of course, I anticipated that the suitors would pay with their lives whether they succeeded or not, the price of paying court to me, but they'd caused me enough angst not to feel any sympathy for them.

People gathered in the city square rather than our own courtyard. Word travels fast. The suitors were all there, and thankfully so was Ulysses, looking inconspicuous at the back of the crowd. I explained the rules. Potential suitors would have to string Ulysses' bow, which had been left in the house, and having done so, shoot an arrow through twelve aligned axe handles or rings. No, I wasn't worried. I was confident that only Ulysses could do it. And if someone else could, it would serve Ulysses right.

The first suitor couldn't even string the bow. He was all thumbs and fingers. He fumbled with the arrow that kept falling from his grasp. He was obviously humiliated. The second was able to string the bow, but could barely lift it, and the arrow went two or three spans before it landed on the ground. Despite his loud protests, he was not permitted a second chance. I had to hold my breath when the fourth man picked up the bow. He was a giant of a man, and was able to string it with ease, but when he let the arrow fly, it was half a span wide of the axe shafts.

What surprised me was the number of men I didn't know who stepped forward, men who hadn't offered me their suit at all. I shouldn't have been surprised. It's so typical of men. Something for free, I suppose. I should have made the rules clearer.

Is there anyone else, one of the consuls called, when a dozen men had attempted the test and failed. And that's when Ulysses emerged from the crowd. No one else recognised him. Probably the beard.

You know the rest. He picked up the bow as if it were another arm, and barely seemed to aim before he sent the arrow through the twelve rings. The crowd was hushed. I think it was the ease with which he did it. Straight through.

Then someone in the crowd, his old friend Diomedes, who'd fought alongside him years before, called out, 'It's you, isn't it? It's Ulysses himself.'

Well, you can imagine the near riot, shouting, weeping, calling out, 'The king's returned.' And of course he had to acknowledge then that it was him. My contest had worked.

But how should I behave? I know exactly what you're thinking. What every woman is supposed to do. Fly into his arms sobbing. 'Oh, my darling. My hero's returned. I've suffered an agony of waiting for you all these years. Oh, how my love still burns as brightly as it did twenty years ago.'

I couldn't do it! He wouldn't come to the house and show me how he'd missed me, utter the words every woman wants to hear. It was time for me to get my own back. I'd prepared for it.

'Oh no,' I told the hushed crowd, who stood in silent fascination as if they were watching a stoning. Isn't that what all the parchments are about? The triumph of romance. Happy-ever-after endings. 'No, that's not Ulysses,' I said. 'Ulysses is dead. He died in the Trojan War. It does look a little like him. Perhaps he's come back as a God.'

The crowd wasn't that easy to convince, but perhaps, just perhaps, I'd made Ulysses realise that he wasn't to take my feelings lightly, or my loyalty for granted.

The celebrations continued in the Symposium throughout the day and into the night. No one disputed Ulysses' right to resume his kingship. Of course there was feasting, followed by the traditional drinking spree at which the men nibbled chestnuts, beans, toasted wheat and honey cakes, all supposed to absorb alcohol, but they never know when to stop, do they? There was also talk of ceremonies of formal welcome.

Most women, when feeling wronged by their spouse, know precisely how much doubt and suffering they should exact from them. They know when the time is right to relent, and exploit their grievance later on, rather than cause harm that they too might regret.

Ulysses had been trying to convince me of his real identity. He explained his movements over the years, and what had delayed his return. He recalled private and intimate moments we'd shared before he'd left, he pointed to the mark on his foot that Eurycleia had discovered when washing him, and I pointed out that if he had returned as a God, he would surely have adopted the body of Ulysses, and would be privy to the personal history of his life in all its detail. Touché.

But it was time, and I planned what I knew would be the final revelation. In his presence, I ordered Eurycleia to move the bed in our wedding chamber. I knew she couldn't. I know, I know. There may have been another motive.

'But you can't,' Ulysses said on cue. 'I built that bed myself, and it's impossible to move because one of the legs is a living olive tree.'

So of course I made all the right noises, told him that my doubts had been erased, called him husband, even wept a little, and that was that.

I sometimes wonder how history will record what I've told you. What stories will be told about it in fifty or even a hundred years' time? How will these happenings be refracted through the lens of the teller? Will Ulysses be the great hero, the saviour of the modern world? Will his Trojan horse be believed, and will his exploits on the battlefield be extolled? Perhaps some of the great writers to come will make something of it. If the enemies of the Greeks write the history, or the stories, he might turn out to be the scourge of the world.

And behind every great man, there's supposed to be a woman. Might I, or perhaps Helen of Troy, deserve a mention, me for my loyalty and sacrifice? Those who write the history have a responsibility to recall, evaluate and reinterpret the past, so that it is intelligible to the new generation. If one of our sex writes the history, perhaps Ulysses will be recorded as an arrogant, vainglorious, insensitive father and mate, whose only claim to fame was shooting arrows through rings, to reclaim the wife he ignored.

# Reunion

A meaty arm held out beside a bulging paunch that tips his studded leather belt half vertical, and wearing sunburn like a farmer's boast, 'It's Rapley, mate,' and when I look puzzled, 'I don't think I've changed that much.'

Our hands still locked together, I struggle to place Rapley. The usual ploy is to remember where they sat in class – what row, how far back, next to whom. At least I recognise the two who are with him. I once regarded them both as good friends, Ellis and Addison. Ellis was a champion tennis player, once lithe and fast, now florid and bloated. We shake hands, Addison grasping mine with both of his.

'It's been a long time,' he says, with a hint of sentiment.

We have a room to ourselves in a leagues club in the west of Sydney. It is the first school reunion of Meadowlands Boys' High School after forty years, and has been a long time in the planning. The old boys are coming from all over the state, and a few from interstate. The early-comers wait expectantly, eager to compare the brunt of the years, to weigh the lives of the half forgotten, if fondly remembered.

'Is Bainton coming?'

'That's not Hawkshaw, is it?'

Most arrive on time and the celebration begins. Small groups form and reform as we move around, surprised, delighted, identifying the older lookalikes, and those who've replaced their schoolboy personas with adult variants.

'Of course it is!' Good-natured laughter. 'I never would have known.' And recognition finalised, it's time to catch some lives, and pin them to the wall.

It's great to see them again, particularly those I might have sworn allegiance to in youthful crusades forty years ago, but part of me is divorced from it all. I feel like a commentator, a biologist of sorts reporting on the span of life from childhood to old age, the ravages of time, the transition from innocence to experience, rather than seeing myself as part of the same narrative.

'Look at him,' my friend since school whispers, and nods towards my old seating companion, now almost bald, and with the hair that remains, a snowy white.

Some of us have already begun to say just enough to catalogue presumed success. Some labour to disprove malignant teacher prophecies. Hevers is one, Hevers who was the butt of Spurling's once a week prediction in physics: 'You have as much chance of passing the Leaving, Hevers, as I have of floating to hell on an iceberg.' It became so much a part of our lesson that, as soon as Spurling started his reprimand, we'd all join in. I think Spurling enjoyed it as much as we did.

O'Brien's treatment of Bracey was more barbed: 'You're an idiot, Bracey. What are you?'

'I'm an idiot, sir,' Bracey said, affecting good humour, but obviously stung.

'I can't hear you, Bracey,' O'Brien smirked, and Bracey was forced to shout his own condemnation.

Of course, most of us were punished at some time or another, so we can only speculate about the scarring left by our schooling. Perhaps this reunion was a forum all these years later to demonstrate our success, or sanity, to our peers. And prove it to ourselves. It had been a time when corporal punishment was in vogue, and sometimes a minor transgression, or none at all, was sufficient to merit the cane or the cuts. There were, though, considerate teachers, and some corrections were more benign. Nicholson, not paying attention, was once told by Miss Watkins to do two hundred lines, and arrived the next day with two hundred ruled lines, and no writing, on several pages. Fortunately Miss Watkins could see that Nicholson wasn't baiting her, and had to turn away to hide her smile. He really hadn't understood.

*

We're a microcosm of the world, this class of '69, the reticent and self-assured, the decadent and those who make integrity a god, the cynical, and those who've struck a deal with life, all of us united in our liver spots and silvering temple hair.

There's much we want to know. What have we all done with our lives? Have we been successful? Are we happy? These are the questions we need answered. And of course most pressing of all is to tell our own story. How do we compare? Our school years were competitive. It was a feature of the times. Triumph in sport was lauded. Exam marks were sometimes presented to the whole class in descending order. Success and failure, right and wrong, good and bad, they didn't allow for as many shades of grey then. Social justice was a seed but the flower hadn't bloomed. We're still competitive. We all have our own narratives to tell. Our modest boasts. Only the criteria have changed.

It's too early yet to share the escalating stories of our mortality, to admit to the cache of pills swallowed each morning or night, to lament the limited mobility, to reveal the blotches on our faces where skin cancers have been removed, to talk of the bike we forget to ride and the broad-brimmed hat we leave at home, to acknowledge the restrictions imposed by type two diabetes. A few are no longer with us. 'Truants', Addison calls them. Their foibles will be glorified by a few who knew them well. Others of us will try to recollect a face by classroom seat. All of this may come later, probably shared by groups of close friends who are able to reignite a long-lost empathy.

I move to where Hevers is holding a group in thrall. Hevers was the tough guy at school, open to accepting dares, boasting of experience that meant one thing for febrile adolescent boys, drinking beer at lunchtime disguised in brown paper bags, and running a book on the Melbourne Cup. We laugh at the irony of his current role as a police sergeant enforcing regulations on both the after-hours selling of alcohol and unlawful gambling.

Bracey is in the group laughing hysterically. The much maligned Bracey, still looking like a character from *Mad Magazine*, and often the butt of bullying, started his career working in a store selling videos and graduated to making them, forming his own video company employing a staff of eight. When quizzed about the subject matter of his videos, and shaking his head at the 'guess-what' selections of his listeners, he smiles when porn is suggested, and basks in what he assumes is daring, and might earn points from his old schoolmates.

Trying to predict potential vocations for people we know is as capricious as trying to select a marriage partner for them. There's a real estate agent, a golf pro, a restaurant owner, a pilot, a lobbyist, a parachuting instructor, and several teachers. All have their stories to tell. Of course, some occupations aren't surprising. Osborne is a natural lawyer, Burton an academic, and Hooper, who ran the student council, a politician.

\*

Years ago we sat, ingenuous and obedient, installed behind our numbered desks, in four serried rows of twin seats, responding to questions rather than asking them, standing when teachers entered the room, raising our hands to speak, prefacing our comments with 'sir' or 'miss', chanting truths that we dare not contest, intimidated by the cane, our minds as impressionable as our tormented bodies with their raging hormones, racked with sodden fantasies.

I think of the faces as they were then, before the metamorphosis that time exacted, the anaemic and serious faces of Sweet and Duggan, an inseparable pair we called 'the brains', the red, freckled and sweaty face of Floyd after playground exertion, the comic and infantile face of Bracey, and the stricken face of Corling when the principal collected him from an English lesson, unusually solicitous for the principal, and told him some terrible news from home. All but a few of those faces stamped with innocence.

Hevers, who is quick to seek me out shortly after his arrival, was the least innocent, but misdeed and mishap are better sources for mythology. Everyone recalls the time he'd had a spat with Cavanagh involving who was the more entitled to approach a certain girl at the bus stop after school. Cavanagh escaped before the bell and, by the time Hevers arrived, had monopolised the girl's attentions. Hevers was furious, and had been looking for days for a way to repay what he regarded as a betrayal.

The opportunity came in a break between a double physics. We sat waiting in the classroom for the teacher to return. Stead was rummaging in his bag, when Hevers, nearby, saw his lunchtime orange with the peeled skin still wrapped around it. Stead knew better than to protest when Hevers took the orange from the bag and discarded the peeled skin. We could all see the juice dripping down Hevers's arm, and we waited with dread and fascination for what we anticipated was to follow.

I remember the classics master quoting Horace: 'I see and approve the better course, yet I follow the worst.' Did Hevers see the better course at all, or did he choose to ignore it? Was it sudden impulse or latent fury that led him on the path to self-destruction? Fate decreed that Cavanagh stand by the door unaware of what most of us could foretell. Fate decreed that Hevers hurl the orange, just as it ordained the science master's appearance at the door as Cavanagh, still unaware, moved away.

The force of the missile knocked the master off his feet, where he lay for half a minute with small pieces of orange flesh spattered over his face, and one eye socket brimful of orange juice.

No one moved. No one went to the master's aid. It later became part of our mythology. We'd roar with laughter at each retelling. But at the time we were terrified. It was calamitous. I'm sure we thought we would all wear the repercussions.

'So why porn?' I ask Bracey light-heartedly after the first round of drinks when the initial excitement of discovery had worn off, so we could share a quiet moment. It's an opener. I don't want to know and don't wait for an answer. 'Are you still doing your famous impersonations?'

Bracey was the class joker. His face alone, almost a perfect sphere, with buck-teeth, and bespectacled with black-framed glasses, made us chuckle. He was good at mimicry, imitating the television celebrities of the time, even the females. Watling, the maths teacher, spoke in a soft voice with an Oxford accent and a slight lisp. He was a favourite target for Bracey's parody.

When Bracey arrived late to class one day, he didn't see Watling sitting next to a student explaining a problem, head down at the back of the room, so, keeping an eye on the door, he strode to the front of the class. 'Now quieten down, boyth,' he began, and continued with his impersonation, exaggerating accent and lisp.

It was of course very clever, and hilarious, but when no one laughed, Bracey became uneasy. A few of us had already resorted to sign language. Sometimes danger is sensed before knowledge takes over. We all remember the smitten look on Bracey's face when Watling raised his head and stood. We feared the worst for Bracey, but Watling, moving to adopt his rightful place, addressed Bracey directly.

'Very clever, Russell,' he said with good humour, 'but I think you overdid the lisp a bit, don't you?' Watling was popular with us ever after.

'Where's Fitzy?' someone asks.

'Didn't you hear?' another answers. There is a lull in nearby conversations. No further explanation is necessary. Memories of the departed are somehow fonder. They tend to be exonerations.

When a few of us shared thoughts of Fitzmaurice over the years, they were always linked with the inconsequential figure of Shand, the geography teacher who carried a small globite school bag rather than the more typical teacher briefcase. Globite bags were solid and rectangular, made for sitting on at school bus stops.

Fitzmaurice, annoyed with Duggan for not letting him copy in the class spelling test, took Duggan's bag, and threw it onto a section of roof in building C. But he didn't realise that Shand's bag was identical, and that he'd taken the wrong one.

A school-wide search eventually discovered the bag on the roof, and a ladder was fetched to bring it down. Of course there were many wide-eyed assertions of innocence when students were interrogated, many convincing 'no, sirs', and many expressions of indignation at the meanness of such an act. No one, though, could outdo Fitzmaurice's display of rectitude.

We knew we were on safe ground, as not every student in the school could be punished, and when we later learned that Shand was a cross-dresser, not that we knew at the time what that entailed, we at least understood that there might be some secrets he was desperate to preserve in the bag.

*

After the exchange of personal histories, the numerous rounds of drinks, and the modest finger food, we assemble for an official welcome from the event organiser, and are read a list of apologies. A hand microphone is handed around for anyone wishing to share a comical school experience. The impact of Hevers's flooring of the science master with the orange, and Bracey's impersonation of Watling, have lost nothing with their successive revisitings in different forums over the years, and are always embellished. On this occasion, the raconteur has the orange as big as a football, Hevers deliberately targeting the master, and claims that the master has refused every offered squeezed juice since.

Also mentioned is the impassioned Reverend Markss, the tiny Anglican scripture teacher who extolled the need for a virtuous life with white flecks of foam flying from the corners of his mouth, and who departed with a smugness that seemed to suggest having wrestled with the heathen and won. Fight the good fight!

I think most of us leave deep in thought with a mix of emotions.

It may be because the lapsing years are beyond reclaim. Were they the best years of our life, or have the perils of age shone a light on all that has gone before? Perhaps this experience has exposed rather than narrowed the gaps between us, between the then and now. Forty years ago, you could have thrown a blanket over the sameness of our lives and dreams. Now life has unobtrusively levered us apart.

Others, like myself probably realise that their legends, heroes and mythologies are no longer shared, that history and culture have colluded through the years to renege on schoolboy memories.

Several hours later, a melancholy Rapley sips a tonic water on his patio. Do I really look as old as most of them, he thinks to himself. Grateful others turn in bed to claim their wives.

# Conferral

'Not like you to miss a two-metre putt,' James commented as the two men headed for the clubhouse.

'It's not really the same, is it, without Charles?' Scott replied, not intending it as an excuse. 'I miss playing as a four, two against two, it's more exciting...and the company of course,' he added quickly, not wanting the permanent absence of Charles to sound only like a sporting inconvenience.

'Hard to take in.' James had been feeling the same. 'Thirty-four, wasn't it, healthy, fit, here one instant, and...' Aware that they'd covered this ground many times in the last three months, the inevitable plainsong of bereavement, he stopped. 'Shall I order drinks now, or will we wait for Adrian?'

'Now I reckon,' Scott answered. 'He's trying to chat up that Barbara in the golf shop. No telling how long he'll be.'

'Does he ever give it a rest?' James shook his head, though not with apparent disapproval.

No sooner had the drinks arrived than Adrian, suave in a green cashmere sweater and beige, tailored slacks, sat down beside them, looking pleased with himself. Adrian, thirtyish, attractive if not handsome, already twice divorced, with several girlfriends but no more permanent partner, was well-liked by his mates because of his generosity and extroversion, even though they openly joked about his 'wandering eye'.

'You look like the cat with the cream,' James said. But, not wanting to hear of Adrian's amorous exploits, 'We were reminiscing again, about Charles, saying we miss playing as a foursome.'

'He's probably up there somewhere,' Adrian was suddenly sombre, 'hitting that three iron from cloud to cloud, looking down on us sympathetically, and thoroughly enjoying himself.'

'It won't be golf for me when I go,' Scott offered after half a minute's respectful silence. 'I hope there's a racetrack up there. And I see myself in a Lamborghini Gallardo, 5.0 V10 engine, 520 horsepower. I'd even settle for a Porsche 911 turbo. That's my idea of heaven.'

'I hope they've got beaches,' James took over. 'A condo on a magnificent surf beach, with the best of food served up on an outdoor veranda, classical music playing all day long, warm days, balmy nights, gold mornings and orange sunsets...'

'Don't expect much, do you?' Scott interrupted and laughed. 'You're getting a little carried away. And what about you, Adrian, though I think we both know?'

'Sex. Unlimited sex,' Adrian, undeterred by his friend's implied assessment, replied instantly. 'I like to see it up there as a haven of the world's most gorgeous women, all available for me to choose from.'

'Thought so,' Scott and James said in unison, and they all laughed.

'Notice how none of us has mentioned golf,' James added, and, lost in thought, they sipped their drinks in silence.

*

With their clothes strewn across the hallway and bedroom, a lubricious smile lay down with Barbara on the marital bed.

'Whatever happened to Beth?' Barbara asked, a brief hiccup in the amorous proceedings. She had known Adrian's second wife, and even in the midst of growing passion, was suddenly curious. Adrian's shoulders might well have drooped if he'd been standing up and not so horizontally nude, but he still managed his best 'She never understood me look. She's not like you.'

Barbara didn't pursue her enquiry. Nothing needed to be said, and the reputation for compassion Barbara owned was served, and Adrian found solace in her generous brand of empathy.

'Oh God!' Barbara's sudden exclamation was less than prayerful. She sat bolt upright. 'It's my husband.'

The car's arrival could be heard on the gravel driveway.

Deathly pale, Barbara leapt from the bed. 'Hurry! Don't just lie there!' Fear mingled with anger as she tried to dress and straighten the bed simultaneously. 'Down the stairs, and out the back door,' she ordered breathlessly. 'It'll take him a couple of minutes to put the car in the garage.'

Adrian was on his feet in an instant. While the scenario wasn't completely new in his experience, a cuckolded husband was always to be feared. He could inflict some serious damage. 'Where, where?' he muttered to himself with growing anxiety. He couldn't find his trousers until he realised they'd been discarded in the hall. He donned his shirt, ignoring the buttons. Just as well, because his fingers were putty. There was no time anyway. He pulled his shoes onto his feet, kicked the socks under the bed, and stumbled to the hall for his trousers.

The garage door sounded, but was it opening or closing? Neither of them knew. Finding his trousers, he pulled them on.

'Hurry,' Barbara hissed, buttoning her blouse and suddenly looking a lot older, as if a lifetime of unwanted challenges had abruptly etched themselves on her face.

Adrian's mistake was putting his shoes on first, because one shoe became wedged in a trouser leg, immobilising him. He had to sit on the floor to lever the shoe from his trouser cuff and free himself.

'Please, please,' Barbara was entreating, more to some divine power than to him, as the garage door sounded again.

They both knew it was closing. Little time left now.

He hurried to the top of the stairs with one leg trousered, the other bare, and his unbuttoned shirt outside his half-on trousers. But he hadn't reckoned on the shoelaces he hadn't time to tie, and tripped in his flight, somersaulting down the sweeping staircase to land in a crumpled heap at the feet of a surprised husband.

'And only the other day we were talking of Charles,' a visibly upset

James commented to Scott as they returned from the funeral a week later. 'One day, he's helping that girl in the golf shop with the accounts, and that's what he gets for doing her a favour…falls down the stairs and breaks his neck.'

'It's just you and me now,' Scott replied, and the two friends believed that circumstance had stamped them with an inseparable bond.

*

'Oh, where in hell are we?' Adrian asked, looking around in the dark and hearing the splashing of oars in the water.

'Not quite,' the old man rowing the boat replied.

'Pardon?' Adrian queried. Perhaps he's a little deaf.

'I thought you asked where we were in hell,' the old man explained, 'and I said "not quite". But it's not far now.'

It was almost black, wherever they were, and Adrian could only just make out the old man's face that moved towards, and then away from him with each stroke of the oars.

'And who are you?' Adrian asked.

'Surely you've heard of me,' the old man replied. 'I thought everyone had. Don't you know your Greek mythology? I'm Charon. Ever since time began, I've been rowing the dead across the River Styx to the infernal regions.'

Adrian fell silent. He was going to hell, and not to heaven. This was his punishment for a profligate life. Fear gripped him. He recalled the talk with his friends about their images of heaven and, with a sense of foreboding, wondered what lay ahead of him. Was it all fire and suffering, eternal damnation?

'What's it like?' he whispered, the words tumbling from his innermost dread.

'It's not just one place,' Charon answered. 'There are many different precincts, and they're all different. It's like your countries and cities in the land of the living. You're the twenty-third I've rowed across today, and no two of you to the same place. Most of them are bewildered like you, wondering why they've been assigned to me, but not to worry. You're in good company. After all, ninety-five per cent of people end up here.'

Adrian remained silent. Repentance wasn't an option now. No use pleading forgiveness. That was only possible in the land of the living. Hell. Wasn't it supposed to be eternal? If so, there'd be plenty of time for reflecting on his shortcomings. The only sound was the gentle lapping of water against the side of the boat.

'Nearly there,' Charon sighed.

*

It's hell. At least I think it is. The legendary Charon rowed me across. But if this is hell, Adrian thought when he was put ashore, I'll settle for it. It's everything I wished for.

The human scape was one of beautiful naked women, some white as ivory, some bronzed like Amazonian warriors. Some were muscular and powerful, and others petite and seemingly vulnerable. There were the earthy women who exuded a breath of the farm and rough living, and the more refined who might have forsaken an Edwardian drawing room. And among this multitude of desirable women, among the surfeit of fleshy breasts and buttocks that stirred Adrian's carnal needs, he could not see another man. So Adrian began immediately to indulge his wish.

No sooner had he arrived than he was propositioned in broken English by a sensual Scandinavian beauty. 'Well, what a lovely surprise. I think you and I should get acquainted,' she said bluntly, and quickly left no doubt as to what acquaintanceship involved.

They weren't all like that. The second was a blushing English woman who engaged in the pretence of wanting to know him, but whose erotic appetites soon came to the fore.

For a fortnight, Adrian was deliciously exhausted at the end of each day despite his prodigious stamina, but he'd wake up each morning excited by the prospect of what lay ahead. And he'd often lie awake in the early morning hours contemplating the style of woman he would grant his favours to when the day dawned. A representative sample, he thought to himself, and laughed. And there was no need for courtly conventions, as the women's need, living an eternity of male deprivation, was transparent.

After several weeks, it became apparent that some women were not satisfied with immediate gratification. They wanted a more meaningful relationship.

'You know you can have me when you like,' Jane, an Australian woman told him, 'but I'd like to think you really cared. I know you'll have some of the others from time to time, and I might be able to live with that,' she continued, 'as long as I know that I'm the most important person in your life, more special than anyone else.'

'But you are,' an increasingly blasé Adrian replied. 'You're my very special someone.'

He told Ingrid, a buxom Swedish woman the same thing, using exactly the same words, and when the two women compared notes, a devastated Jane withdrew, despite her earthy needs.

It was ironical that after several months' glut of sexual activity, Adrian began to long for something deeper, if not more permanent for himself. He re-established his soured relationship with Jane, telling her of his need for a real relationship, admitting that his sole physical and erotic desires had evolved into a deeper psychological need. She was delighted, and they began to provide each other with the small indulgences that each grants the other in a relationship. They spoke at length, related their personal histories, and played on the banks of the Styx.

But as their relationship deepened, the sexual dimension also increased till Jane, after an eternity of abstinence, was impossible to satisfy, and exhausted him with her demands.

He approached several other women, seeking friendship only. 'A platonic relationship,' he explained, and of course they concurred, but as soon as the friendship grew, the women wanted more. And he continued to be confronted by the carnal needs of scores of starved women who came from across the precinct to avail themselves of the lone male.

So Adrian began to long for the friendship of men. He craved the sexless bond of male companionship without the lure of sex and fraught desire, free from the injured feelings and the games that multiply. For the first time since his arrival, he thought of James and Scott, and their regular games of golf, and he knew that the feelings he once confessed to them were to another self.

For the first time, Adrian understood that this was a living hell.

*

He remembered Charon telling him that there were many precincts in hell, like there were countries and cities in the land of the living. Hadn't he rowed twenty or more people the day he was ferried, and each to a different place? There must be plenty of men in hell. They deserved to be there as much as women!

His life had become unbearable. The women came to him by day using every manner of ruse to elicit his favours. They came throughout the night, each with their own agenda, but each having one particular item to be acted upon. If there were other parts of hell, he wondered, parts with an even number of men and women, how could he get there? Charon's arrival and departure were invisible. He could hardly swim the Styx. There was no telling where he might end up.

He asked several women if there was a way for him to go elsewhere. They were horrified by his intention, and imposed a ban throughout the precinct on revealing the information. But eventually he was able to bribe one of them who exacted a considerable payment in kind. It was worth it.

There was a woman, he was told, and she alone could make such decisions. She must have been some sort of high priestess. 'Your fate,' his informer told him, 'is entirely in her hands.'

Adrian was buoyed by the news. There was a way out after all! He was given instructions on how to find her. It was difficult to make the journey unnoticed because while he wasn't under surveillance, he was rarely left alone. And he couldn't disguise himself as a woman because they were all naked.

But he did manage to flee in the early hours of a morning when the hell fires were only smouldering and not giving off much light. He had little trouble finding 'She', the simple title the women gave her, a tall dark woman of unparalleled beauty with a voluptuous figure, waist-length hair and regal bearing. For the first time since his junior school days, Adrian was momentarily tongue-tied.

'Well?' she said, the terse invitation for Adrian to put his case.

'I've enjoyed my time here,' he stuttered, believing it diplomatic to begin positively about his experience. 'But...' and he recounted his longing to be among other men.

'She' asked for more detail of his experience in hell, and listened attentively, watching him closely and paying particular attention to the accounts of his sexual adventures. When he'd finished with a final plea, her face seemed to reassemble as if some layer, some officious accretion had been rinsed away, leaving a tenderness more typical of her sex, and as she beckoned him to approach, she opened her arms, and her lips parted in a seductive smile.

He knew then that all was lost.

Acknowledgement to A.D. Hope, *The Damnation of Byron*

# Words

Miss Prine: Thank you for coming, Mr and Mrs Enright. It's far easier to have this sort of talk in person, rather than over the phone.

Mike (combatively): And what sort of talk is that, Miss Prine? And please, it's Harriet and Mike.

Miss Prine: Well, you must know it's about Tim, Mr…Mike.

Harriet: Oh dear, he's such a good boy, Miss Prine.

Miss Prine: Look, I won't take too much of your time, but Timmy has been using some very inappropriate words in class and in the playground.

Mike: And what exactly are these words, these inappropriate words?

Miss Prine: I'm not going to repeat them. But let's just say they are about the lavatory, and about sex. Timmy's in fourth grade now, and he really should know better.

Harriet: But he's such a good boy, Miss Prine.

Mike: Are you quite sure about this? It isn't just some of the other children talking, making up stories the way they do.

Miss Prine: I'm afraid not. I've heard him myself, and on more than one occasion.

Mike (resolutely): Thank you for telling us, Miss Prine. I'll have a word with the boy, and we'll sort all this out.

Harriet: He's such a good boy.

Miss Prine: Please do so. If it goes on, if the other parents…then it will have to go to Mr Slade.

Mike: Rest assured Miss Prine. I'll be talking to the boy, and if what you say…

Miss Prine (testily): Mr…Mike, I can assure you it is true.

Harriet: He's always such a good boy.

Miss Prine: I have to ask this. But is there anything at home that might be upsetting Timmy? Is he under a lot of stress? I've noticed that he's not playing with the same friends in the playground. Is he worried about other boys? Sometimes an argument, sometimes the arrival, or expected arrival of a new brother or sister.

Mike (indignantly): Miss Prine, I really hope you're not insinuating that we are not doing a good job parenting our son.

Miss Prine: No, of course not. It's just that there's always an explanation. He might be showing off. Sometimes the boys don't know what some of the words mean. But I needed to bring it to your attention. It needs to be nipped in the bud.

Mike (defensively): One thing's for certain, Miss Prine. He's never heard any bad language in our home!

Miss Prine: I think we've said enough. You have a serious talk to Timmy, and hopefully it will cease to be a problem. Thank you for coming in. I'll keep you informed.

Harriet (feebly): He's really such a good boy.

*

'Well, what did you think of Miss Prine?' Mike asked a very disconsolate Harriet when they left.

'I didn't really warm to her,' Harriet answered weakly. 'And I'm sure she's wrong about Timmy. She said she heard him use bad words, and more than once.' She looked at her husband imploringly. 'You don't believe her, do you?'

'Yes and no,' Mike said reflectively. 'Yes, I'm sure Timmy has probably used a rude word occasionally. Boys hear things and repeat them, probably in the playground out of bravado…just think of what they hear on television nowadays. I'm quite sure I said a few things I wouldn't be proud of when I was at school.' He paused for a while to think.

'And no?' Harriet prompted.

'No, I don't think it's as bad as our Miss Prine is making it sound,' Mike replied. 'I'm quite sure the other boys are just as guilty. They're probably just better at not getting caught.'

'Surely if he used those words, we would have heard him,' Harriet whispered, feeling that the doors were being thrown open on her protected life. 'What will we do, Mike?' Harriet had a long-standing problem with anxiety, and she was wringing her hands, looking to her husband helplessly for a definitive answer.

'Exactly what we told Miss Prine we'd do,' he replied. 'I'll talk to Timmy. Perhaps it will all become clearer then.'

Timmy was expecting a confrontation. He'd seen his mother and father at the school, and after the warnings he'd been given by Miss Prine, he could guess what it was about. His natural defensiveness relaxed in the face of Mike's low-key approach, and indirect tactics.

'Your teacher's a little concerned about you, Timmy,' he began. 'Are you worried about anything, about the other boys, about your mum or dad, your studies?'

'No, Dad.' the reply was immediate.

'I'd sometimes use rude words when I was at school,' Mike resumed with the 'this is really quite natural' ploy. 'And that was OK, unless it was done too much, and it upset people.' He paused. He had danced around the issue for long enough. Timmy knew what was coming. 'Do you know what I'm saying?' Mike was more blunt now.

'I've never used any rude words, Dad. Not at school, not anywhere, not ever. Never.'

Mike persisted. 'Of course, sometimes a word might have a different meaning to the usual one, depending on where we use it, or how we use it.'

Timmy had to think about this for several seconds to allow the meaning to become clear.

'Years ago,' Mike elaborated, 'your mum would sometimes call me "a little rat", and it meant that she really liked me. It was like a joke. I was her little rat. She sounded really affectionate when she said it.'

'Yes, Dad.' Timmy brightened as if a light had just been switched on. 'I meant just that when I called Simon, Oliver and Sarah arseholes.'

'But Timmy,' Mike remonstrated, 'you told me before... Oh, never mind.'

Shortly after the talk, Mike rejoined Harriet, who was lying on their bed suffering a migraine.

'Well?' She sat up so suddenly, the pain was excruciating.

'It's just as we both thought, darling,' he eased her back onto the bed. 'I'm sure we have nothing to worry about.'

*

'The truth will out,' Mike reckoned. A serial offender cannot resist the impulse for long. If Timmy made a habit of swearing, or using rude words, it would soon reveal itself. And it did.

Mike worked for a very large accounting firm, and every spring there was an annual picnic at the same local park. The executive correctly surmised that such an occasion, at which members were encouraged to bring their families, was good for staff morale, and therefore improved productivity and teamwork among the workers. As an aspiring member of staff, ready to take the next rung on the promotional ladder, Mike was eager to impress.

The firm had arranged for caterers who picked their way among the few park tables and the many rugs spread on the ground. The food was in the best of taste, and there was ice cream and sweets for the children. Families mingled. New friends were made. At the appropriate moment, the boss welcomed them all, extolled family togetherness, and presented staff with novel awards that were greeted with howls of delight – the messiest desk award, the Luddite award for the most technologically unsound, the appeasing award for the best at handling customer complaints. The children were ushered to another section of the park, where they were enraptured by a professional children's entertainer, and then permitted to run free.

That's when it happened. Timmy's choice selection of words in his piping and aggrieved voice was heard by most of the gathering. Unchecked, and seemingly unfazed by his initial indiscretion, Timmy soon after launched into another string of foul language, and this time, it was directed at the boss's daughter.

Mike, torn between chasing after Timmy and chastising him in front of his now silent colleagues, or ignoring it, and hoping it would 'go away', was transfixed. Harriet promptly announced another migraine.

*

Mike: I hope you don't mind me contacting you, Miss Prine, but I admit I was a little suspicious before, about Timmy, I mean, but I know now that you were right. I apologise.

Miss Prine: It's good that you've come, Mike. I was going to call you this very day. Did you have that talk with Timmy?

Mike: Yes, but I don't know that it did a lot of good. Has he been any better at school, or is he still…

Miss Prine: I'm afraid to tell you, Mike, but it has got worse. A couple of teachers on playground duty have noticed. One or two parents have come forward, made complaints. They say it's upsetting their children, and are demanding that something be done.

Mike (flummoxed): I'm not, well, I don't know, what do you think, what…?

Miss Prine: I'll have to take it further, Mike. I've tried. I sat down with Timmy and did my best to explain, told him it upset a lot of people, the other children, the teachers, his mum and dad…but because there have been complaints, it will have to go to Mr Slade.

Mike (after long deliberation, ingratiating): I know I have no right to ask, but I have an idea, something I'd like to try. Would it be possible, Miss Prine, to give me a week? Just one week is all I'm asking. If it hasn't improved by then, we could meet here next week, and you could tell Mr Slade.

Miss Prine (considering): Perhaps a week isn't out of the question. It's really against my better judgement…but if there's another parent complaint in that time, I'll have to report it. My hands are tied. There could be big trouble for me. I'm so sorry, Mike.

Mike (relieved); I really appreciate it, Miss Prine.

Miss Prine (gently): OK, Mike. A week. Oh, and Mike…it's Elspeth.

\*

Mike went to Timmy's room that night after dinner, trying hard to appear nonchalant. 'Just checking on how school is,' he said and, getting a non-committal answer, started to move away, but pretending that he'd just thought of something, entered and sat down.

Timmy didn't know of his visit to Miss Prine earlier that day because he'd been at sport. Harriet didn't know of it either.

'You know your mum and I were really upset when you used those words at the picnic.'

Thankfully, Timmy seemed to be chastened.

'We must have heard about ten or twelve words that you shouldn't use because they hurt people. Most people think they're really rude. I think you know what "offensive" means. I'm not going to say them now, but I only hope there aren't any more.'

'No, Dad. Sorry, Dad.' Timmy showed a rare glimpse of contrition. 'It's just that I get so mad sometimes. A lot of the other kids get me so furious, and that's when I say them, the rude words.'

'I know. I get mad too,' Mike identified. 'Some of the men at work annoy me, but I've learned that it's best to say nothing. I used to say rude words, but I taught myself to keep quiet. Do you think you could do that?'

'I'll try, Dad,' Timmy said without conviction.

'Good boy,' Mike enthused. 'You could even start by not saying some of the words, and every day refusing to say one more until there are none left.'

Timmy considered the proposition.

'But whatever you do, Timmy, there's one word you must never, never under any circumstances, say. I'm telling you this because you might already have heard it, and use it without thinking. It's the world's worst word.'

Timmy's interest piqued. His father said no more, so Timmy had to ask, a little tentative, 'What is it, Dad?'

Mike made a show of considering whether or not to tell. Then he went to the door to check if anyone was within earshot, and returned to sit on the bed and whisper. Timmy leaned forward to hear.

'It's "parsons",' and he feigned a mild shudder. '"Parsons",' he said again. 'There's "pee" and "arse" together, and when coupled with a "nose", it means a chook's backside.' Mike didn't stay any longer. The revelation had been momentous. He left it hanging in the air. And he left Timmy brooding in silence.

*

Miss Prine: Well, I have to hand it to you, Mike.

Mike (expectant): An improvement then?

Miss Prine: Improvement's not the word for it. The swearing, the rude words, they've stopped altogether.

Mike (incredulous): Nothing at all? Just like that? (Clicking his fingers.)

Miss Prine: For a couple of days, I could see that he was getting really annoyed in the playground. He didn't say anything, and he seemed exasperated, as if he were holding it all in. And then when Dominic kicked his soccer ball into the infants playground, he said something to him, quietly, but it wasn't a swear word. It wasn't rude. And he's been behaving the same way ever since, saying the same thing. If looks could kill...but those words we used to hear have gone.

Mike (obviously pleased): That's more than I hoped for.

Miss Prine: I won't ask you what you said to him, or whether you put the fear of God into him, but whatever it was, I'm getting worried (laughing). You might be taking my job soon.

Mike: Thank you for what you've done, Elspeth. For giving me another chance.

Miss Prine (tenderly): Mike, if there's ever anything, anything…

(Mike leaves with an ironical smile broadening to a grin.)

# Donegal

Donegal first spoke to Tom one bleak November afternoon. And from that moment, Tom was well aware what people would think. This fellow thinks a dog can talk. But he was prepared to suffer it all – the nods in his direction, the whispering behind cupped hands, the fingers initially raised to point then respectfully diverted to rub a nose or scratch an ear.

And it wasn't the fertile imagination of the doting mother who swears her infant said 'Dada' when it merely gurgled. Donegal's first words were erudite and deeply resonant. 'The literature review was superb, but her treatment of the methodology was slight. I'm not sure she understands Miles and Huberman.'

Tom had been marking an Honours thesis, and Donegal's comments rang true.

'Yes, I can talk,' he answered Tom's incredulous stare. There was mischief in those doe soft amber eyes, and he began to laugh good-naturedly, his meaty tongue lolling back and forth like wipers on a car. The twilight sun splashed into the room and lit his copper fur.

'But you never spoke before.' Tom hovered in that zone of disbelief, waiting for fantasy to declare itself. But there was no one else at home. It was no hoax.

Donegal uncurled himself from the floor, and strode upright to the armchair, where he sat down cross-legged. 'I haven't felt the need till now,' he said reflectively. 'Besides, it becomes galling for an intelligent Irish setter to remain silent to "Donny wonny want a bikkie" or "Donny want to go walkies."'

'I'm really sorry, Don...Donegal.' Tom sensed the absurdity of his apology and went no further. Then he felt sad and guilty. This was an intelligent…creature who understood the qualitative analysis of Miles and Huberman, and who'd been relegated to leashes, nightly walks, raw bones and a kennel.

'Don't worry about it, Tom,' he smiled. It's hard to gauge expressions from such a proboscis, but there was no 'master', or 'Mr Ellis', but 'Tom'. Names position relationships. They define role and status, and this was a signal of equality. 'Can I get you a coffee?' And before Tom could answer, he strode to the kitchen, filled the kettle, and began to apportion coffee and milk in two mugs.

That night, Tom emptied the junk from the spare room. 'I want Donegal to have his own room,' he told his disbelieving wife. 'A soft bed to sleep in, a table to work at, and his own books.'

His wife was very caring for the next few days, diverting the children, bringing him breakfast in bed, insisting that he sit and read or watch television while she stroked his forehead, and even walking Donegal. Tom felt sure that Donegal gave him a complicit wink that first night as he trotted off compliantly.

As an academic, Tom was trained to not accept things at face value. He wasn't alone with Donegal in the house for a few days, so he used the opportunity wisely. He researched the ways words are produced from the speech organs, the modification of air moving under pressure from the lungs by the vocal cords, soft palate, teeth, alveolar ridge, hard palate, tongue and lips. He discovered how the palatal fricative x is sounded when the front of the tongue is raised near enough to the hard palate to create audible friction, and how the velar fricative occurs when the back of the tongue is raised near enough to the soft palate. It just wasn't possible! And he studied comparisons of human and canine brains, the function and relative sizes of cerebellum, cerebrum, hypothalamus, corpus callosum and corpus striatum. No, it wasn't possible! But the next few weeks, and years, would challenge such scientific certainty.

*

The 'coming out' of Donegal was a cautious and deliberate process. First there was the family to convince.

'Now I don't want you to think I'm mad,' Tom began, and realised he'd planted a prolific harvest.

What else could they think? But Donegal came to the rescue, demonstrating the range of his talents. The children were delighted. They had another brother, ready-made, playful and not demanding parental attention. Donegal was sensitive, indulgent and patient. His guile in bowling leg spin and the flipper would sometimes irritate Tom's son if he was dismissed with successive deliveries, but Donegal proved a master of diplomacy.

His wife was a different proposition. As a mere dog, Donegal was lovable. As an intelligent male of indeterminate age, he was suspect. It might have been his manhood, more manifest now that he insisted on walking upright, that unnerved her. Perhaps it was the shift in power. You can cuddle a child. Its desires and needs are malleable. But you can't as readily fondle a grown male, particularly when there is no consanguinity as defence.

While she supported Tom in his plans for Donegal, her relationship with him became more restrained. Her affection wasn't as demonstrable, and she spoke to him with the urbanity you afford a visitor rather than a family member. She never walked him again, and yet for that Tom was secretly grateful. One of his fondest memories was running with Donegal. They'd go at night so Donegal could run upright, and they'd discuss the latest novels of Saramago, Marquez and Philip Roth. But there was never a time that his wife wanted Donegal at the table when they entertained friends for dinner, even though he was the perfect model of decorum and could explain the culinary predilections of all the royal courts in Europe.

The second phase in Donegal's coming out was to reveal his secret to a wider circle. To the chagrin of Tom's wife, it polarised their friends. Some thought it marvellous. It appealed to either science or the absurd. Tom's close friend, a devotee of Bertrand Russell, was delighted, claiming it turned the world on its head. Others were disturbed that it challenged a cherished natural order, and one woman was disgusted. 'A dog is a dog is a dog' was all her intellect allowed. 'If you think I'm going to sip cucumber soup at the table with a, with a…' and they never saw her again.

Donegal was equal to the adulation and denunciation. He seemed above it all except for one black day.

The husband of a lifelong friend of Tom's wife was crudely decrying the lack of female talent in his workplace. 'And as for Yvonne,' he mocked, 'she's a real dog.'

Donegal's copper fur bristled. His eyes lost their sheen. Tom could see his tension as he sat next to him sipping his Chardonnay.

'I think you'd better apologise,' Donegal said icily.

'Don't worry, mate,' the man laughed. 'It's a figure of speech, just an expression.'

Tom still nurses an image of the man's flight down the river-pebble drive at Dural, with an upright Irish setter, eyes agleam, brandishing a baseball bat in hot pursuit, and gaining with every stride.

*

Donegal sat for the Higher School Certificate with Tom's son. He did the same subjects by correspondence, though he did have to formally sit the examination. There was some consternation among the invigilators when Donegal took his seat, arranged his pens on the desk and donned his reading glasses. One girl was carried from the room shrieking with uncontrollable mirth.

Universities accept candidates to degree courses by HSC percentile scores. So it was that Donegal was accepted into teacher education at the university.

Again there were hiccups at enrolment. 'But you're a dog,' the wide-eyed woman said at the enrolment station.

'Yes,' Donegal replied matter-of-factly.

'But,' the woman was flustered, 'it doesn't say so on the application form.'

Donegal took the form deftly in his paw. 'You're quite right,' he said officiously, 'and there's no place for anyone to indicate whether or not they're homo sapiens. In fact…' Donegal pressed home his advantage, 'there's nothing here to indicate whether applicants are porcine, canine, feline, equine, bovine, wolverine or simian.'

Equity provisions were firmly entrenched at the university. Applicants couldn't be excluded on the basis of race, background, gender or disability. There was no formal provision to cover Donegal, though the spirit of the policy was clear, and a dog-loving vice chancellor decided to take the risk.

Incredulity, caution, novelty and acceptance were the stages in Donegal's adoption by the students. After initial bewilderment, they began to talk to him, tentatively at first and then wholeheartedly. It became desirable to work on group assignments with Donegal or to sit with him in the refectory. Even when the novelty had gone, Donegal's great compassion and brilliant scholarship made him a favourite.

Practice teaching proved the stumbling block. The day started badly and grew worse. Tom arrived at Lindfield Public School with Donegal, upright, a new leather briefcase in his paw. A dog-catcher had just locked a nondescript terrier in his wire-caged utility. Tom saw the dog's furtive glance at Donegal, the downcast look of the victim, and felt unusually sad.

'Bloody circus dog, is it?' the dog catcher called, looking pointedly at the 'No Dogs on Premises' sign and back to Tom before he turned to his ute.

'Up yours, feller,' Donegal growled in a tone that belied his usual equanimity.

'What did you say? What did you bloody say?' The man approached, puce and bellicose, fists clenched, and standing with his face centimetres from Tom's.

'On yer bike, feller…or I'll bite yer backside.' Donegal was enjoying himself.

The man swung round to look at Donegal. Then he wheeled to

look at Tom…and back to Donegal. Right, left, right to cross reality's divide. 'I'll bloody well…I'll bloody…' And lost for words, he retreated.

The school principal was a gentle soul, but terrified of crossing the departmental line. 'I really can't put you in a classroom,' he explained, at least affording Donegal the courtesy of direct address. 'If the Department says it's all right…' and an urgent meeting was convened with the Department that afternoon.

Soames was a malevolent man who thrived on creating obstacles. He'd pore over precedent or legal definition, and take gratuitous delight in promoting uncertainty and pain. As life had clearly not been kind to him, his retaliation was indiscriminate. A magnificently groomed and handsome dog with a Boss briefcase, and demonstrable culture and erudition, was a new challenge. Difference was to be feared; superiority detested. 'There's a regulation,' he was snide, 'about animals in schools. You're clearly an animal,' and he savoured the word.

Tom and Donegal parried by reading the equity provision in the *Teachers' Handbook*, and the anti-discrimination legislation.

Soames was not deterred. 'There's a regulation,' he whined, 'about school staff wearing appropriate attire. If I'm not mistaken…' he was revelling in his cleverness, 'you don't have any attire at all. Not to put too fine a point on it, you're nude.' The word was pronounced 'nyood', and with all the relish of the infant boy's incipient use of 'bum'.

Donegal remained calm and with not the slightest hint of self-consciousness. 'The significant word, Mr Soames,' he retorted politely,' is "appropriate". It would be most inappropriate for a dog to dress. If he were to do so, he'd be accused of aping humans, if you'll excuse the pun. If you wish to enforce that regulation, you'll be vilified by Animal Liberation.'

'There's a regulation,' Soames began again, unmollified.

And so they traversed the minefield of Department regulations governing professional image, duty of care and relationships with staff and children. Soames even threatened to consult an actuary. If every human year, he argued, is equivalent to seven dog years, then

Donegal would have to pay seven times the normal superannuation contribution, and that would leave him no salary at all.

Donegal didn't become a teacher, at least not in a school. But his months of work were not for nought. His reputation for scholarship was such that the university offered him a research position that also involved a small teaching allocation. His output of research papers was prodigious, and his talents as a teacher were vaunted.

\*

'You look really tired, Don,' Tom said. They'd been watching *Madame Bovary* together after the family had retired to bed.

Donegal was sitting on his reclining chair, his legs apart and his nose erect. His eyes had rolled back to reveal their whites, and the glasses had fallen from his snout. He'd been snoring, a low gravelly rumble.

'You've been pushing too hard.'

'No, it's not that,' he replied wearily. 'There's something I have to tell you.' Donegal wasn't one for proclamation. He was normally so understated that Tom sensed the portentous.

Gobs of rain dashed the window from a galvanic sky. There was the tell-tale eerie silence that precedes revelation.

'I'm not young any more.'

Tom smiled. 'Not young. You're only eight.' He was relieved and even dismissive.

'No, let me go on. I'm older than you. I'm fifty-six. I am tired. I have arthritis in my tail, and standing erect has played havoc with my lower back. I reckon on four good years...four of your years. The last year at the university's been great, but I have to make fresh plans.'

Tom felt an extraordinary sadness. There was a slight greying around his snout. His teeth had muddied a little and his amber eyes were a paler honey. Tom had faced his own mortality, but never another's, and it was hurtling towards them. Tom wanted to hug Donegal but didn't move. Was it his own very humanness, the veneer of seemliness that held his instincts in check? Was it Donegal's barely quasi-humanness that curbed his response? Or was it Donegal's greater benignity that gave Tom pause? What he felt for him now ran deeper than master and loyal servant. He was wise counsel and compassionate friend.

'I want to devote the rest of my life,' Donegal continued, 'to my own kind. I've been selfish. Now it's time to give other dogs the chances I've had.' He could see Tom's pain and lightened the mood. 'Every dog has his day,' he quipped and laughed.

'Why not let sleeping dogs lie?' Tom challenged. And so they retired to bed.

After one of those nights when the mind permits the body no rest, Tom rose early and went to Donegal's room with a litany of questions. He wasn't there. The bed hadn't been slept in. And he wasn't downstairs cooking breakfast. 'Donegal,' he called. There was no answer. 'Donegal.' After the third call, Tom saw him emerging from the kennel on all fours. 'Donegal.' Tom ran to him. 'Is everything all right?'

There was no answer.

'Aren't you going to speak to me?'

Donegal wagged his tail and ambled to the nearest azalea to lift his leg.

Tom made the usual breakfast of bacon and eggs. Donegal showed no interest and would only eat the dried dog food of yesteryear. He didn't go to work and he didn't return to his room.

Later that day, Tom fetched his old leash, hopeful that he would confide on their nightly run. He didn't.

He never spoke again. He never walked upright. Instead, he disappeared during the day and often overnight, returning dishevelled and exhausted. Even as the months became years, Tom didn't relent, using their times alone to speak to him. At first, Tom inquired, pleading for affirmation. Then he simply offered his support: 'If there's anything I can do,' or related the events of his day at university: 'You'll never believe what MacFarlane did.' Tom still doesn't know if he listened. He certainly gave no impression of doing so.

*

The day Donegal died was bleak and grey like most July days. The pallid morning was thawing with anaemic colour. Tom found him sphinx-like in the kennel, his head on his paws, and his eyes vacant. At least he was grateful that Donegal was spared capture and summary execution.

The family gathered to bury him that morning in the backyard. That's what he would have wanted. Tom remembers bundling him into his arms, and staggering with his weight, his copper fur ablaze in the winter sun, and his legs splayed like palings hanging off a fence. The family stood around his grave, and they each said a few words. There was no invocation of theology or talk of doggie paradise.

The family members went on each of their weekend ways, and Tom remained alone for what he knew would be a time of painful self-indulgence and catharsis. He had to confront the profound sense of loss he couldn't explain. He needed to feel his feelings, and allow the pain to spill his understanding. And there was guilt to resolve. Surely he could have done more.

The storm arrived mid-afternoon, heralded by black scudding cloud that switched off the sun, and lightning that knifed the dark. Tom thought it biblical, nature's underscoring of the momentous. The initial ferocity abated in several minutes, but the rain continued to fall heavily.

There was a faint scratching at the family room door, and through the glass Tom could see a forlorn-looking cocker spaniel, sodden and shivering. Inside was safe haven. He opened the door and closed it quickly against the elements. She stood in a growing puddle of water on the entrance tiles, not daring to shake herself. Tom went for a towel.

'Thank you so much,' she said with a dulcet voice. 'Beastly weather.'

And Tom knew the visit was no accident.

# Juror

'But I am anxious about it,' said Simon, 'particularly now you're telling me there are no clear markers. Surely there has to be a set of criteria, something to go by.'

On Stirling's forced retirement for an undisclosed indiscretion, Simon, with a reputation for his selfless charity work, and an untarnished reputation in public service, had been appointed by the committee as the fourth judge, and was determined to do justice to the role entrusted to him. He'd certainly had his doubts, but this was a fresh challenge.

'Some things can't be quantified,' Price answered with barely disguised disapproval.

Simon's appointment upset the apple cart, and threatened an entrenched modus operandi, one that had worked well for years with the same four.

'I understand there has to be a great deal of subjectivity,' Simon persisted, hoping he didn't sound pedantic, 'but that doesn't mean there can't be criteria. Apart from scientific research, every field involves judgements, interpretations, but they always have some yardsticks…refereeing a football match has rules, interviewing for a job has requirements that have to be satisfied…' He stopped, realising he'd said too much too soon.

At this stage in the conversation, Rourke, one of the two other judges, entered the room, and Price introduced him. Rourke was a handsome, dark-complexioned man in his early forties with exaggeratedly fleshy lips, a supercilious air, and eyes that were constantly roving rather than settling on his audience. Price, the head of the judges, was older, greying around the temples, and, unlike Rourke, possessed a stare that made you feel like an exhibit, squirming on a pin. Bellamy, the fourth judge, wasn't there yet.

'Simon wants to know how we judge,' Price told Rourke with a knowing and critical look. 'He wants to know our criteria.'

Rourke smiled, put his hand on Simon's shoulder in a manner that seemed more condescending than fraternal, and asked Simon what he meant by criteria.

'Last year,' Simon began, more determined now to make his concerns known, 'Miss Venezuela won the Miss Cosmos Beauty Contest with a score of 78.75 per cent, and that was 0.25 more than Miss Sierra Leone, the runner-up. You, I believe, were the judges, so all I want to know is how those scores were arrived at. You have to agree that's a pretty fine distinction you made.'

Price and Rourke looked more serious, perhaps because Simon's questions were an implicit threat.

'Basically,' Price began, 'it's sex appeal, and I don't mean that in a salacious way. It's hard to be specific. We do try to ensure that we agree, that there aren't big differences between what we all think.'

'Wait till you see the girls on stage,' Rourke came to Price's defence. 'Some of them have a certain *je ne sais quoi*,' whether it's how they look, how they move, what they give out.'

'But they're all in swimming costumes,' Simon persisted. 'All in one-piece costumes, so is it just a matter of determining the *je ne sais quoi* as you call it? Is it just waiting to see which girl each of us finds the most sexy, in a nice way of course? Surely it's not just a matter of ogling bottoms and bosoms and legs? And talking of ogling, I have to say I find it strange that there are no women on the panel.'

Price was irritable now. This was bordering on defiance. 'And for a good reason,' he said tersely. 'Women are blinkered when it comes to judging their own sex. Men can be more objective. You're making it into something a little distasteful,' he added.

Rourke was more sensitive to Simon's concern. 'It's really a matter of connoisseurship. We've been chosen to do this because we have a highly developed appreciation of the finer things in the human condition. You ought to be flattered that you're now one of us. And don't forget, each of the contestants is interviewed, so that is also taken into account. We're able to get an overall picture.'

'That's right,' said Price, buoyed by Rourke's assumed success in convincing Simon, 'connoisseurship, and it is a role that comes with its tangibles.'

'You mean intangibles,' Simon queried, thinking of the privilege and status associated with the role.

'No,' Rourke smiled, 'he does mean tangibles. Bellamy's in the hotel now with Miss Costa Rica, working on the tangibles.'

*

The girls were on stage in the massive auditorium of the Hilton, the hotel where each of the contestants was staying. The pageant's organisers were putting the girls through their paces before the main event to ensure that everything ran like clockwork. Although dressed in street wear, the girls didn't miss a chance to impress. Many didn't know which of the sundry people beyond the stage, some busy barking instructions, some attending to technical details, and others simply watching the trial run the day before the contest, might be in a position to influence the result.

So street wear comprised skintight satin pants, the briefest of shorts, and skimpy see-through blouses that left little to the imagination. Make-up was painstakingly applied. Connoisseurship. The word came to Simon's mind as he watched from the back of the auditorium.

He must have looked an unlikely judge, because a group of the girls had ignored him at breakfast that morning, after his first night in the hotel. Miss Ukraine had told him to watch where he was going when she had nearly run into him carrying her coffee. Would she have behaved differently, he thought, if she knew who I was. Would she be mortified, desperate to make good?

He had realised that there was no use pushing Price, Rourke and Bellamy further about how to score the contestants. He would sit near Price when it came time for the judging, and take his lead from him. He was still concerned about the lack of criteria. It was contrary to all his training, but there were already three or four of the girls he was drawn to, and he was at a loss to define why. Was it that *je ne sais quoi* quality that Rourke spoke about?

And so he watched the girls rehearse as television cameras were positioned, light and acoustics tested, and glittering signage put in place.

'Now again!' a surly organiser called, and the girls paraded in circles, some entering and retreating in file to the left and some to the right.

One said something to the girl in front, who muttered under her breath. Another feigned a half kick at the girl in front she believed was too slow and who might shield her from the cameras tomorrow.

'Remember,' the man shouted, 'the cameras will capture everything. Every look, blush, grimace, every fear and doubt will be seen by millions. Now again! Get it right this time,' and he hummed the music as a cue for the girls to parade. 'Miss USA, you're to the right of all the others. Miss France, too sexy, you look as if you're going to seduce the audience. Miss Italy, too flamboyant, tone it down. Miss Belgium, you're too colourless. Smiling yet regal. Smiling and regal.'

\*

'Welcome, everybody, to the Miss Cosmos Beauty Pageant, an annual event when the most beautiful girls in the world are gathered together to see which lucky contestant in a few hours time will be wearing the crown of Miss Cosmos, the world's most beautiful woman. This telecast is being beamed to a hundred and ten countries.' Danny Starlight, ageing celebrity and host, beamed into the microphone, under the blinding stage lights, his brilliantly white teeth flashing as if they were wired to a battery, his wig painstakingly groomed and sprayed. 'In a moment, you will see all the girls parade. Girls from every continent of the world. Then you will meet each of them in turn. Six finalists will be selected…'

Simon watched as the girls began their parade, tanned in cut-away swimming costumes of various colours, some with a faint, coquettish toss of the hair, all with deftly jouncing female parts and saccharine-studied smiles, rehearsed resilience in their movement, striving to be just a little different from the other forty-seven girls, but without flouting convention and earning the ire of organisers. Miss France and Miss Italy still managed to appear slightly more animated than the others.

The full parading complete, Danny introduced the contestants one by one, lingering over the name of the country. 'Miss Argentina.'

Simon was overwhelmed by her beauty and sexiness, or was it only the latter he wondered, as she smiled with understated seductiveness, and walked slowly around the stage in her red costume from which she threatened to burst, legs lengthened to advantage in high heels and a costume that, at the side, rose above her hip. Completing the circuit, she approached the microphone, where Danny, all panache, asked the usual searching questions.

'What are your hobbies – what do you like to do?'

'I like to help other people,' she replied with switched-on seriousness. 'I love to help animals. I read and I like to go skiing.'

'Thank you, Miss Argentina.' Danny flashed his dentures again, and Miss Argentina moved slowly away, determined that audience and judges alike could see the bottom that her boyfriend said was one of her best assets.

There was half a minute's pause before the next contestant was to enter, and Simon looked at Price's computer screen where he had entered the mark. Price, realising that Simon was a neophyte in this skilled business of connoisseurship, was happy to reveal his score. This kind of confederacy was to be valued. Simon, detecting some subtle message conveyed in a look between Price and Bellamy, decided to award a few more percentage points to Miss Argentina. Each juror was conscious of appearing imperturbable, as they had been warned the television camera could capture them at any time.

And so the forty-eight contestants were introduced and scored.

Miss Australia smiled warmly with a girl-next-door look and paraded in green and gold, honey-brown limbs, a little less boldly than Miss Argentina. 'I like to care for those less fortunate,' she looked at the camera with ingenuous eyes. 'I have a lot of animals, I take strays in off the street. And I like reading and skiing.' She was one of the several contestants that Simon found attractive, and he typed in his score without looking at Price's computer, much to Price's displeasure.

Even though each contestant was only allowed a few minutes, it took some time for each of them to parade. Danny didn't wilt, but seemed to try even harder to upstage each girl with his exuberance, and began to lean into them more obviously. His wig had begun to slip and looked awry, and as the girls left the stage, dragging the attentions of an appreciative viewing audience behind them, an assistant would quickly wipe the beads of sweat from his forehead before the camera panned back.

Occasionally, he'd ask a different or supplementary question. When Miss Costa Rica entered, there was another barely perceptible look exchanged between Price and Bellamy.

'And what do you spend time doing?' Danny enthused.

'I like helping others, and I love animals. Sometimes I go skiing.'

The consummate host, Danny believed she needed to be drawn out. 'Who do you think are of some of the great people who have changed the course of the world,' he asked. 'People like Gandhi and Mandella?'

She looked puzzled for a moment but quickly recovered. 'I don't follow the football,' she said.

\*

'I think I'm getting the hang of it now,' Simon told his three fellow jurors. The six finalists had been identified, and his colleagues didn't seem dissatisfied with the decision. As Danny was speaking, and was therefore the focus of the telecast, Rourke gave Simon a hidden thumbs-up, a signal of approval.

Miss Australia and Miss Costa Rica were both in the finals. Simon admired the restraint of the contestants during the drawn-out process of announcing the six, as all forty-eight stood waiting anxiously in a half circle as rehearsed, but he couldn't help wondering about the disappointment they masked by gracious smiles and gentle applause, probably pondering how so-and-so could possibly be deemed more worthy.

Sometimes their ease was betrayed by just the hint of a crestfallen look. And a few disappointed contestants, still wearing their forced smiles, managed to cast fleeting looks at the faces of the judges, who sat on an elevated platform at the base of the stage. Bellamy studied his screen and didn't look up.

I suppose it's inevitable, Simon thought, that even with the strictest criteria, we all have our favourites. In any relationship, some people excite, and others, even those with demonstrably better looks or greater personality and talents, don't. Price and Rourke are probably right. Could any criteria suffice? It's only to be hoped that the *je ne sais quoi* quality might be shared by more than one of the judges. That would make the process more valid.

Simon had enjoyed the experience, had accepted the limitations of judging, and decided that he would be available for the contest in years to come. He might even be eligible for some of the tangibles that Bellamy seemed to enjoy, whatever they were.

There was a short break in the proceedings before the six finalists were reintroduced. They had not as yet been ranked, and stood in a row, smiling, models of grace and decorum. Even though the decisions had already been made, and would be announced excruciatingly in reverse order from sixth to first, they were required to parade once again, and to endure further questions from Danny, who had worked himself into a feverish excitement. Excitement because the hometown girl, Miss USA, was among the finalists and, when announced, had received the most applause from an unashamedly partisan audience. Miss Australia, Miss Costa Rica, Miss Bahamas, Miss Portugal, and Miss Iceland were to parade and be questioned again. Was it deliberate that Miss USA was last in line?

Each of the girls parades again, and seems to have grown in assurance, so much so that the audience in the auditorium, and the millions of television viewers around the world, are convinced that the judges have chosen correctly. The girls move with greater style and speak with greater fluency.

As Miss USA begins the final parade of the pageant, the men in the audience ogle her, stewing fantasies, and form mental imprints for later retrieval of her shape and texture. Her parading is complete, and there is a hush as she approaches the microphone and a salivating Danny. A question is asked, and in the close-up camera frame, there is a captivating look, both charming and sincere, as, gently drawing breath, she lifts her head and moos.

# Seduction

Seduction, like love, is a chameleon word. It changes colour to match a variety of expressions. To be seduced by a wonderful orchestral performance has little to do with a sexual desire for the musicians. To claim that you've been seduced by someone's argument simply means you find it particularly persuasive.

Scenarios for seduction, in the more usual sense of persuasion to engage in sex, may be casual and impromptu affairs when the hormones of one or both participants are aroused; they may be long, meticulously planned rendezvous with an anticipated end; or they may evolve from a more natural, romantically inspired realisation, born of an unexpectedly kind circumstance that both parties involved might even find surprising. Theirs was the latter.

It was an ideal scenario. They sat on the lounge together, he tall, painfully thin, even gangling, leaning ever so slightly against her smooth and yielding body. The lounge was deep-cushioned, the sort you can sink into. An apricot-shaded lamp shed a warm glow where they sat, a pleasant and subdued lighting. Piano pieces from one of the European masters was gentle across the room, pleasingly audible, but not so loud that it interfered with talk. All was silent outside. Theirs was a world within a world, a clichéd scene that literature extols both to move a plot to complications, or to satisfactory conclusion.

'I've never really been popular with girls – women, I mean,' he told her, turning to watch her face that expressed an intent look, benign. 'Perhaps they might find me more attractive if only they could understand me.'

He was immediately embarrassed because this could be interpreted as a plea that he was feeling sorry for himself. How much should I reveal, he wondered. Perhaps I shouldn't pour out my soul. It might frighten her away. But I feel so comfortable, more comfortable than I've ever felt before.

\*

What accounts for comfort, he mused. Well, obviously being able to be yourself. But what did that mean? Nietzsche had an expression that might explain it: *Werde der du bist.* We become what we are. Have I become what I truly am, he asked himself. Is that why I'm feeling so comfortable with her now?

It hadn't been that way before. Denise made him feel uncomfortable. Very uncomfortable. She kept implying that he was gauche, even telling him so, and telling others as well. She always found little things to niggle him about. 'You're so painfully slow when you drive,' she'd say. 'Why are your reflexes so slow? What are you waiting for?' Even something as simple as writing a letter would be criticised. 'What a weird signature. Will they know who it's from? Why don't you put the stamp squarely in the corner rather than obliquely like that? It's so slapdash!'

When they went to dinner at her girlfriend's, who now dated one of her old boyfriends, he was teased mercilessly, but there seemed to be a sharp edge to her teasing.

'I warn you, Celia, you'd better watch him. The last time we went to dinner, he managed to spill the red wine all over himself, and the tablecloth and carpet. Mr Clumsy, we call him.' And later in the evening, 'I don't think he'd be much good defending me if I were attacked. He might be blown over by the wind. Now, if it were you Brian...'

Was it all in good fun? He wasn't sure. But he was sure about not feeling comfortable.

But the worst time was a winter's day when it was howling outside, and they found themselves approaching the possibility of intimacy.

They seemed to move against each other, their heads clashed, caresses were wooden.

'What's wrong with you?' she said in exasperation, getting up, heading for the door, and calling back over her shoulder, 'Mr Clumsy strikes again.' That was the end of that.

*

We all live with so much that we repress, he thought. Can we ever faithfully convey to someone else who we are, what we feel, what makes us tick? For the first time, sinking with her in the lounge, in the apricot glow of the lamp, and with the piano murmuring softly across the room, he felt he could say yes.

'Let me tell you a little about me,' he said to her. 'Then I want to hear all about you.' He began with his childhood and his rearing as an only child in the large stone house at Epping with his two old-world parents. He spoke of the difficulties he faced during adolescence and early adulthood, when he was diagnosed with a chronic medical condition. He told her of his tertiary education and the passion with which he pursued his job as a clerical assistant. And he even felt comfortable enough to elaborate on his earlier claims that he had never really had a satisfactory relationship with a woman. He thought that would lend support to his current devotion.

But what was more important was the exposé of his feelings. Descriptions of situations and events reveals a little. Reporting feelings is what really divulges the inner man. And so he spoke of his feelings of torment, frustration, elation, loneliness and pain. He happily disclosed his vulnerabilities. Beethoven's piano CD clicked to a finish and restarted, and still he kept talking.

She didn't interrupt once, but watched him intently. She obviously wants to understand me, he said to himself. That must surely be a mark of what she feels. It's a gift to listen, and to listen without judging, and without having to interrupt with your own agenda. Not like Enid.

*

'Logorrhoea' is defined as 'uncontrollable or incoherent talkativeness'. He'd discovered the word in the dictionary. That was Enid. She was a very large woman with the jolliness that is sometimes associated with overweight people and that is often expressed in uproarious laughter, but she did have a soft heart. He was at first beguiled by her constant talking to him, that he interpreted as comfortableness and interest. But she rarely stopped talking, and often he simply wanted silence, a space of calm where he could rest his addled brain, order his thoughts.

When she invited him to dinner to meet her parents, he couldn't get a word in edgeways.

'What work do you do?' her father asked.

'He's a clerical assistant with Spencer and Spencer,' she answered. 'And a really good one. Only last week the boss praised him, said he had a real future with them...' and so it went.

'What interests do you have?' her mother asked.

'Well, this is interesting,' Enid replied as his mouth had half-opened to reply. 'He collects fossils from everywhere, sends away for them, and specialises in the bones and teeth of vertebrates. He plans to write a book one day on the calcareous exoskeletons of invertebrates. And he likes bushwalking. I do too, so that works out really well, doesn't it?'

He realised the futility of the relationship later, even though he desperately wanted someone to fill the void in his life. It was the day he was interviewed for a significant promotion.

They'd arranged to meet immediately afterwards, and rather than inquire about the interview, his feeling of elation was doused by 'You'll never guess what happened to me today. I was to meet Beth for coffee, and when I got there, Sylvia and Tyne were there and said why don't we all go shopping, and so we went to David Jones, and I bought a lovely pink top that I'll show you later, one that's a loose fit with puffed sleeves, and Sylvia bought a pair of black slacks with sequins up the side. You could be a model, the shop attendant said to her, and

115

I thought to myself that might be true but her bottom is too big, and Tyne is better model material, and I stubbed my toe getting on the escalator and Sylvia said that I could sue them for that and get enough money to go to Hawaii.'

He didn't see her again.

*

The piano accompaniment came to a halt with a click and didn't resume. It was suddenly silent, but pleasantly and non-threateningly so. It was black beyond the penumbra of soft orange light. They were leaning against each other, sunk in the recesses of the lounge.

The talk had been an aphrodisiac, particularly as he had revealed his true self, and his vulnerabilities, free from pretence or praise-seeking. She hadn't been critical of him, or judged him like Denise. Nor had she denied him a voice like Enid.

This was probably the most significant event of his life. A revelation both of himself, and of her – a likely soul partner. With this realisation came desire. He put his arm around her, and met with no opposition. So he turned towards her, and sat more upright from his semi-reclining position on the deep-seated lounge.

He always anticipated that he would have to rely on a cue from a woman in assuming any liberty like this, so reaching around to hold her with both arms, and fiddling with the fastener behind her back was new territory. Seemingly well received.

He felt the clasp release, felt the expectation that rushes to meet likely eventuality, and was already anticipating his next move when she collapsed, melting into his arms with that same benign and unerring gaze, and a sound that was shrill and whirring. He'd bloody well let out the air!

# Georgie

Georgie Porgie, pudding and pie
Kissed the girls and made them cry
When the boys came out to play
Georgie Porgie ran away

Old nursery rhyme

George Porter acquired a number of nicknames from schoolmates in his youth, but the most enduring was Georgie Porgie, no doubt deriving from his infants' school exposure to nursery rhymes, and his like-sounding surname. In his adult years, 'Porgie' was dropped except by one or two old school friends who used it as an enduring mark of affection.

Born in Adelaide in 1945, George, whose generation was dubbed 'the baby boomers', enjoyed a modest post-war affluence. He lived in a newly established, leafy middle-class suburb where all families enjoyed a comparable lifestyle, and so avoided invidious social comparisons. His father was an accountant, and his mother didn't work, freeing her to help on canteen, attend the ladies' auxiliary at the local school, and to assume a gentle protectiveness over George and his sister Susan.

His infant years were a timeless blur, timeless because the only markers were night and day, and for Georgie they weren't part of any bigger scheme of calibrating life, and in between wasn't measurable either. Lunch, when he asked his mother, might be 'soon', whatever that meant, or 'not for a while yet, Georgie, you've only just had breakfast.'

Sometimes, his parents went out at night, his father in a black suit, a starched white shirt with little buttons and a stiff collar, and a bow tie, and his mother in a shiny dress that caught the light and held it, with her hair all done up, and smelling like the jasmine that hung over the cubby where he played with Susan. He'd hug his mother before she left, calmed by the coolness of her touch, heady with her perfume.

On those occasions, he'd be taken with Susan to Grandma Hilda and Aunt Enid, who lived in a big federation house around the corner. He'd be given a pink musk stick and a fizzy orange drink, played snap and sevens, was put in a big double bed with Susan, and was later carried to the car by his father in the early morning hours when it was still black and cold. 'I was awake,' he'd tell his mother in the morning, as if it were a mark of being grown-up. 'Susan wasn't,' he'd say.

Memory favours the unusual, ignoring the sameness of days, yet latching onto the special occasions like birthdays and Christmases with chocolate icing and lit candles on a cake, plum puddings containing threepences and brandy sauce or ice cream, and the presents he methodically arranged on his bed to admire, and to show Susan and his parents.

There were other unusual or memorable events too, like the day his father brought home Monty, a Dalmatian puppy; the awful day Grandma Hilda passed away and he wanted to know where she'd gone; and the time he and Susan both fell when a tree branch they had climbed on in the backyard snapped. Both his knees and one shin were badly grazed and bleeding. Susan suffered a heavy bump to her thigh that would probably become a bruise. Their mother came to the rescue, concerned that Susan may have broken something, and fetching cotton wool swabs and Dettol to bathe Georgie's wounds.

Susan sobbed. 'It hurts, Mummy,' she kept saying.

'I know, darling,' Mother soothed, 'but it'll stop hurting soon. You'll see.'

Georgie tried as hard as he could to be brave, yet his legs hurt, and the blood was trickling into his socks. And as suffering is often infectious between children, he began to whimper, a sign of imminent tears.

'There, there,' his mother patted his head affectionately. 'Little soldiers never cry.'

\*

Georgie's school years at Belmore Primary, a state school, offered little excitement. In the 1950s, the consummate teacher was regarded as one who could break learning down into manageable chunks and present it to the students in a palatable form. Students sat in serried rows, raised their hands to answer questions recalling information rather than seeking opinions, parroted information, learned by rote, often to the tapping of a ruler, and kept quiet unless addressed. A full-class lockstep curriculum assumed the children had the same ability and application, and ignored individual differences. Failure to learn was the result of laziness or not paying attention, and incurred the wrath of teachers.

For Georgie, school was something to be endured. He'd rather be with Susan in the cubby, or playing cards with Grandma and Auntie. Even at a tender age, he had some inkling that it was a rite of passage to an adult world. He was a good student, but had little comprehension that school had any instrumental value, that he could learn something he could later use. It was more a technical exercise, a proving ground.

Yet there was some worthwhile learning, if not prescribed by the curriculum. He learned that obedience was the requisite for getting on; that teachers and some other adults have a mortgage on all knowledge; that respect is demanded rather than deserved; and that standing up for oneself was essential for playground survival.

But even that proved problematic. Katie Nicholls became his bête noire. Georgie learned early on that girls didn't behave the same way as boys. But he hadn't yet learned the caprice of emotion. Didn't understand why a girl spurned might become a committed enemy. Hadn't reckoned on Keith telling others about the note that Katie had given him, swearing him to secrecy, a note that spoke of kissing him in the dark. Kissing was daring enough, but that it should take place in darkness added something thrilling, even forbidden.

Ever since she discovered his indiscretion, Katie had turned sour. She'd scribbled in his composition book, stolen his pencils, told the other girls in the class that he smelled like an old sandshoe, and made up stories about him.

Georgie was annoyed with Keith for telling, and his embarrassed attempts to make good with Katie fell on deaf ears. 'I do like you,' he told her, but her hurt was too deep.

So the sight of Georgie in the playground, laughing with the very popular Julie as if they were the very best of friends, was like a red rag to a bull, and she hurried towards him, called his name so that he turned round, and hit him hard in the face. Georgie's mistake was retaliating. His instinctive return slap was met with a few seconds of stunned silence before she began to scream. Julie stood open-mouthed. Other children watched in fascinated silence.

Georgie was hauled to the principal's office. 'But, sir,' he protested, sick with fear, 'she hit me a lot harder than I hit her, and I didn't do anything to cause it. Mine was just a little slap.'

Katie was not called on to give any account at all.

'You never, never hit a girl, Porter, not under any circumstances. Do I make myself clear?' the principal said sternly, reaching for his cane.

*

Sarah was with him when he opened the fateful letter that would change his life. It was 1965, and his birthdate had been drawn in the lottery for all twenty-year-old males, requiring him to serve two years full-time national service. The National Service Act had so ordained in 1964, and he was to be in the first intake.

Sarah, his long-time girlfriend, had been a constant companion through his senior school years. Their friendship grew from the time they were both fourteen, and their peers viewed them as inseparable. They studied many of the same subjects, sat together in most classes and, living in the same street, were able to spend time together at weekends without the hassle of taking public transport. It was only in the last year that they both attained their licences. And they managed to do so on the same day.

Following the initial shock of the letter, they discussed more soberly what he could do, sought advice from local dignitaries, and scanned the dissenting literature advocating draft dodging, but there seemed to be no way out. Conscientious objectors could be gaoled, and Georgie was not likely to fail the medical.

The few months leading up to his departure for training were emotionally tortured. His father, a recently returned ex-serviceman, was concerned; his mother was distraught, particularly as it was announced that national servicemen could be sent to South Vietnam to fight in units of the Australian regular army.

The night before he was sent to Puckapunyal in Victoria for his twelve weeks of training, he spent with Sarah. Long, tormented silences were broken by haemorrhages of impassioned promises as they clung together.

'I'll write every week,' Sarah vowed. 'I know it will be difficult for you, but I know you'll do what you can,' and, as if to endorse his going, 'I'm proud of you, Georgie.'

With their passion fuelled by love under siege, and the possibility, however remote, that he might not return, they gave themselves to each other. It hadn't been anticipated, and it was their first time. Afterwards they lay side by side, sensing the creep of separateness return, willing it not to, feeling infinitesimal, in awe of the world's mystery.

Unused to regimentation, Georgie found the training gruelling and demeaning. It sacrificed autonomy to unthinking response, eliminated privacy, and except for a few superficial friendships based on shared anxieties, he had little in common with the other recruits. Sarah was true to her word and wrote regularly. Georgie, homesick and lovesick, lived for her letters and was able to write a few of his own.

While his training was degrading, his experience in Vietnam was a nightmare. The war was not straightforward in policy or strategy. The Vietcong fought a campaign of insurgency, subversion and sabotage using guerrilla warfare tactics. Sometimes it was difficult to determine where the enemy was, or who they were. Friends were killed outright or cruelly maimed from booby traps. One of his companions from recruiting days shot himself in the tent they shared. Mud, jungle, insects, stifling heat, constant reconnaissance and surprise attacks were his life for eighteen months. There was no communication with the outside world.

Still dressed in military uniform, he returned after his two years a shadow of his former self, no longer a mere boy, but a damaged man. His parents hugged him at the front door, and his mother sobbed and offered thanks aloud in prayer.

'Sarah?' he whispered his enquiry at the door, his return home having been unannounced, and his mother, having feared this moment for weeks, took his arm and led him to the lounge, knowing she could not delay or cushion the news that Sarah had married two months earlier.

*

It was a slow recuperation, and although Georgie continued to have the occasional nightmare, he managed to put most of the horrors behind him, and to cope with the poor reception the returning soldiers received. Avoiding the usual analgesics of alcohol and drugs that dulled memory as well as pain, he went to university, graduated in history and became a tutor in the faculty.

One year leaked into another, and he became more assured and robust. He enjoyed his teaching, was praised by staff, and was popular with his students. Naturally conservative, he adopted the seventies fashion of flared trousers, body shirts and multicoloured seersucker ties.

After three years of tutoring, a lectureship fell vacant in the faculty, and as the position required expertise in his own area of specialisation, he had reason to believe it had been tailor-made for him. 'It's got your name on it,' his close friend and colleague enthused. 'You've served your apprenticeship, done the hard yards...'

But Georgie didn't get the position. It was given to a woman who'd been tutoring in the faculty for fifteen months, who had a slight curriculum vitae, and who was not a favourite among the students. His friend, outraged, encouraged him to appeal the decision, but Georgie was reluctant to do so until he understood why. Disappointed and nonplussed, he went to Munroe, the faculty dean, who also chaired the selection committee.

Munroe was both embarrassed and sympathetic. 'Believe me, George, I understand your disappointment,' he began, anticipating Georgie's obvious questions, and in a rare moment of disclosure, 'I'd be furious too if it were me.'

'But Trevor,' Georgie began, 'if she were the better candidate…'

He wasn't allowed to finish. 'I can't really comment on how the panel saw the merits of the two candidates,' Munroe said, 'but let me say this,' and he moved around from behind his desk to sit with Georgie, a show of confederacy, 'hypothetically of course. Sometimes it's not always a level playing field. Let's say for instance,' and he paused as though he might be conceding too much, 'let's say the government or university gives a directive about positive discrimination…and sets quotas…the need to have more indigenous or disabled, or it might even be females on staff,' and he looked pointedly at Georgie, 'then perhaps the hands of a selection committee might be tied.'

*

On the way out, Munroe's secretary, obviously privy to the goings-on of that office, intercepted him. 'I'm really sorry, George,' she said. 'I can imagine how you must feel, and I know,' she whispered confidentially, 'Trevor was really annoyed about it.'

Pleased by what seemed to be genuine sympathy, Georgie lingered. 'There's nothing I can do,' he half commented, half questioned. 'I've been told I should appeal, but from what Trevor implied, that will do me no good at all.'

'I don't imagine I would if it were me,' she tried to soothe. 'I'm not an academic, but I don't think it's you either,' and as an afterthought, 'It might create more trouble than it's worth.'

'You're a real lady, Emily,' he said gratefully, testament to her discretion, and saw her eyes lose their light.

'No need to call me a lady,' she said icily.

'I'm sorry.' Georgie was confused, but could see that she wasn't joking. 'What should I call you?' he offered tentatively, the years of military subjugation still alive.

'Woman. I'm a woman,' she replied testily, and resumed her duties without another word.

\*

Georgie Porgie, pie in the sky
Won't kiss the girls, they wonder why
When the girls come out to play
Georgie Porgie runs away

# Identity

'Quick, he's finished.' The executive member in the front row nudged his colleague. 'Get Jimbo to wake up.'

Jimbo had slid sideways by degrees until his head was resting on the shoulder of the man next to him and, much to that man's irritation, was emitting loud adenoidal snores.

'You were nodding off yourself. And I think I've lost the will to live. Will you give the vote of thanks, or will I?'

Seymour gathered his copious notes and stood down from the rostrum to barely audible applause from a few polite members of the audience.

Mrs Bellamy stood in the doorway to the meeting room, hands on hips, and raising her eyes to the ceiling, mouthed 'an hour and a quarter' then, approaching the executive member in the front row, lamented that the lunch would be well and truly spoiled.

A friend of Seymour's had told him that he should try motivational speaking. Was it from irony or malice? So Seymour had advertised his talents, and had consequently been asked by a branch of the public service to address them on 'How to Make My Work Performance Dynamic'. This was his first, and turned out to be his only, foray into motivational speaking.

'I'm afraid there's only fifteen minutes for lunch, ladies and gentlemen,' the executive member announced to groans from the bleary-eyed gathering.

Seymour was a bachelor in his mid-twenties, and lived alone in a small two-bedroom apartment. Tall, spare, with a shock of dark hair, and not bad-looking, he wasn't given to physical pursuits. He worked in the local library, enjoying the cataloguing of books, and while there were only a few part-time work colleagues with whom he could interact, he did have a small group of loyal friends that he had retained from his school days.

One of them referred to him as 'a stay at home sort of guy', because Seymour was happiest moving between his home and the library that he'd often visit in the weekends when he wasn't required to work. He didn't join his friends at tennis or rugby, and he certainly wasn't a pub-goer, preferring more cerebral recreation, and he rarely took a holiday. When he did, it was usually only a few kilometres from home.

His consuming passion was conchology, or the study of mollusc shells. 'Oh no,' his friends would whisper when an unsuspecting stranger was polite enough to ask him whether he had a hobby. 'I'm a conchologist,' he'd say. 'Do you know that we conchologists investigate four different molluscan orders. There's the gastropods or snails, the bivalves or clams, polyplacophora or chitons, and scaphoda or tusk shells. Now, a shell gives a lot of insight...' and the stranger would wave to an imaginary person across the room, mutter 'Excuse me', and retreat. 'I'll explain more when you have time later,' Seymour, oblivious, would call after them.

It was a similar story if Seymour had just been to the cinema. The innocent question 'Was it any good?' would be answered by a detailed and deadpan twenty-minute description of the plot, with some verbatim repeating of dialogue. And his eyes would hold the solitary listener like a steel trap.

He'd never had a real relationship with a girl. There'd been dates with a few women, but never more than one. If he asked for a second date, the girl was invariably out of town, indisposed, or having to work late. One used the ruse that while she preferred his company, she couldn't afford to antagonise another boy who 'had eyes for her'.

Yet it didn't seem to worry him. He'd enjoyed the dates, particularly the chance to talk about conchology and the classification of library books. For Seymour, there was nothing to be suspicious about. One girl, who had thought Seymour seemed a nice enough bloke, and had been on a date with him, reported to one of his friends that watching grass grow was more exciting.

*

'No man is an island.' Not even Seymour. He had a small group of old school friends who were willing to indulge his strange ways. They were friends who believed in the true value of friendship, and understood that they all had a responsibility to each other. That meant lending a helping hand when needed, even if it were painful to do so, and making sacrifices if necessary.

'Should we be doing anything at all?' one asked. 'After all, he seems to be happy with his life, with the way he is. Why trespass on that?'

'Is he really happy?' another countered. 'Surely he must see the effect that he's having on other people. If he doesn't see it now, it might hit home harder later on, when we mightn't be around to help, and then he's doomed to a lonely future.'

'And it's not so much whether he's content,' said a third. 'He, and perhaps we, must consider others.' After several minutes of debate, it was decided that they should talk to Seymour.

They did so at his apartment, and after several minutes of dilly-dallying to no effect, the leader of the group decided he needed to be blunt to get the result they desired. Sometimes you have to be cruel to be kind.

'People see you as boring, Seymour,' he said. 'It's not so much the things you do by yourself, it's the way you behave with others. You talk and talk and talk, and it's dull and people don't want to hear, not in that much detail anyway. They want to run a mile to get away.'

'I always thought everyone was fascinated by my conchology,' a disheartened Seymour replied.

'I think what we're trying to say,' another friend took over, 'is that you need to be yourself. Just relax, be yourself. You seem to be keeping it all bottled up. You don't have to do all that talk to prove yourself. Relax. Just let it all hang out.'

'But how do I do that?' Seymour queried uncertainly.

'Just look at Justine,' a third friend explained. 'She lives life to the full. She's uninhibited. She's not afraid to joke and tease and laugh out loud, to be the first to get up and dance, to take risks that could land her in trouble, to explore what life has to offer, even to wear revealing clothes.'

'Of course you don't have to do all those things to be yourself,' the fourth friend added.

Half a minute's awkward silence followed. They all shifted uneasily in their seats.

'I know you have my best interests at heart,' Seymour commented, appearing crestfallen, and his friends departed quietly with mixed feelings.

'I'm not sure we've done the right thing,' one commented.

'No one likes to be told that the world thinks they're boring,' said another.

'He just needs time to think,' said a third friend, 'time to take it all in. It is for his own sake.'

*

'Purple, I think,' Seymour said.

'Are you really quite sure about this?' the hairdresser asked.

'Yes, that or lime,' Seymour answered with conviction.

And so his impressive shock of black hair was dyed deep purple.

He was squeamish when the time came to have his ears pierced. He'd spent half the day looking for the right earrings, and settled on some very large orange hoops to complement the colour of his hair. 'Don't be a sook,' soothed the eighteen-year-old girl performing the procedure, and it was done without incident.

Enduring that gave him the courage for the next step in his plan. This, he predicted with relish, would really wow them.

'I'll be a while,' the man in the parlour said, not looking up from his work tattooing a long prose message on the broad canvas of a woman's back, a woman who lay naked from the waist up on a massage table.

Seymour looked around the small airless room, one wall of which displayed the photos of tattooed rugby league players, and the other that featured tattoo designs. Stopping for a moment, the man waved a hand at the graphic art on the wall, and at a large, spiral-bound book that contained suggestions for tattoo messages.

Seymour took his time, intrigued by the man's work and fascinated by the possible inscriptions in the book. He considered 'I am I am I am', and 'Celebrate this chance to be alive and breathing', but settled for the tattoo of 'Be the one to guide me' on his right thigh, and 'But never hold me down' on the left.

After the purchase of a new wardrobe, Seymour reckoned it was time for his coming out. It began slowly and not auspiciously. At an official function, dressed in silver lamé, he sang the national anthem in loud, Tiny Tim falsetto, provoking the ire of the assembly. And at a small gathering of would-be comedians performing for the first time in a smoky restaurant that he visited with his friends, Seymour would laugh, a strange hyena laugh, immediately before the punchline, infuriating the audience and performers alike. The management asked them all to leave.

In a cohesive group, one member, if sufficiently well liked, is able to build up idiosyncrasy credit. That person can move away from the normal and acceptable behaviour of the other members, providing they don't roam too far. Seymour did.

It was a birthday party for the sister of one of his friends. The room was full of young people, some uninvited. The music was loud. Alcohol was on tap. Seymour, dressed in his tight-fitting gold lamé, his purple hair combed back, moved from one group to another, stopping only to refill his glass, telling the same joke and rehearsed anecdote, and laughing noisily. There was no talk of conchology or the classification of library books. He made a beeline for any girl who was sitting by herself.

Late in the evening, a girl began to dance by herself to some Latin American music. She was a shapely girl with panache, and moved in perfect time with the music. People had stopped to watch.

'Is that who I think it is?' Seymour asked one of his friends.

'Yes, it's Justine,' his friend answered.

Justine. Justine. Oh, he knew that name all right. The incomparable Justine.

Without waiting for her to finish, Seymour climbed onto the table that had only recently been piled with food, and was now littered with used paper plates, plastic cups, and crusts of pavlova, and began to dance, if dance was a fitting description. It was more a succession of jerks and uncoordinated movements unrelated to the music.

Justine stopped dancing. She had lost her audience. All the partygoers had flocked around the table instead. Faces were alight with expectation. People were laughing and egging him on. Some of the men lifted their glasses and toasted him, and called out for more.

This was a new experience for Seymour. Conchology may have interested people, but it had never given him this attention, or adulation. So, thrilling to the calls for more, he managed clumsily, without having to sit down, to peel off his gold lame trousers, revealing the tattoo high on his thighs. 'Be the one to hold me, but never hold me down'. How apt that seemed now, he realised, and kept thrusting out his left thigh. Hearing all the murmurs from his audience as to what the tattoo said, he pirouetted slowly for all to see, and removed his jacket and shirt to display a white and slightly hollowed chest. With the occasional male shout for more, his movements became more exaggerated, and even obscene.

At what point does the funny become sad? At what moment can adulation creep towards indictment? His audience began to move away, some with simple disinterest, others with a pitying shake of the head. Yet still Seymour kept dancing, a lone and pallid figure, ridiculous in his underpants.

*

It was time for another meeting. His friends had conferred before visiting Seymour for a second time in his home.

'That's not exactly what we anticipated,' one said.

Being uninhibited like that doesn't mean you're being yourself,' said another.

'I'm partly to blame,' said a third. 'I told him about Justine.'

Seymour was delighted to see them, expecting approval for the new man that had evolved, but their sombre looks should have told him otherwise.

'Are you really being yourself?' one asked. 'Do you think that is the real you?'

Seymour was disappointed, and perplexed.

'Do you think, Seymour, that you've been trying too hard to be something or someone you're not?' another said.

'Was that the real Seymour we saw at the party?' the third friend persisted. 'The funny dancing, the stripping, showing off your tattoos and purple hair. Did you feel comfortable? Did you feel...it was you?'

'You need to know, mate, that we all care about you,' the first man resumed, as Seymour didn't answer. 'We all want what's best for you. I suppose what we're trying to say is that you don't have to be outrageous to be yourself. Look at each of us. We play sports, we have an occasional drink, we like to have a good time. People can be...uninhibited and quiet, and still be themselves.'

Seymour's friends left, partly from feeling like executioners, and partly from diplomacy, because they knew Seymour was disappointed and might need time to take stock. Not a word was exchanged between them as they went their separate ways.

Seymour retreated to his bedroom, and stood looking into the mirror for a long time, trying to read his face, searching for any meaning it might reveal. Were his shadowy eyes the window to his soul? His purple hair was fading and showing dark roots. I should get it dyed again, he thought to himself. Or should I? Then he opened the cupboard door, and looked at his gold and silver lamé outfits. They were a little rumpled and not sparkling now in the unlit room. A single orange hoop earring looked weirdly incomplete on the dressing table. The other had been lost during his bizarre dance.

What should I do, he asked himself. He was so confused. Is the new me, me, or is the genuine me, the me that used to be?

# Retrospective

We used to call the old trains red rattlers. I suppose the bus that dropped us at the school gates should have been called the green rattler. Or the green and yellow rattler. We kept thinking it would fall apart, churning up those hills and wheezing around the corners. I must have parked two, three hundred metres away today, but of course the school's a lot bigger now, and many families didn't even have a car all those years ago.

It certainly has changed. That used to be one big dirt playground at the back of the school, and we'd kick a ball around at second half lunch, two teams of about thirty boys, come into class sweating and with a gauze of dust on our shoes, sometimes wipe them clean on the opposite sock. We all wore shorts. Now the playground's full of demountables. That's the name for temporary classrooms, or rooms that can be picked up on a truck and plonked down at some other location. The population of the suburb is changing. Lots more kids now. And a lot more migrants.

Grandparents' Day. I have to say it's a great idea. Says something about the value of us older people. An acknowledgement that there's knowledge and wisdom that can be passed down. Gives the young ones a sense of the continuity of the generations, and the understanding that one day they'll be like us. Nothing like that when I was here. Teachers felt that parents shouldn't meddle, or be a part of the school's business. We didn't learn anything like it in class either. Now the young ones get a greater appreciation of what those who came before them did, particularly those who fought in the war. History is modern as well, social science. Not just the explorers and governors, the First Fleet.

Hello, boy, what's your name? What a handsome kelpie you are.

Come on, give me the ball. Come on. Want to play? All right, don't then. Wouldn't be the same would it, a kelpie like you without the telltale hairless tennis ball wedged in your mouth. Walk with me then, feller.

Slade had a dog. Could we ever forget it! Can you imagine a school principal now being allowed to have a dog at school? Bones. Strange how we name things. Call fat people Skinny, tall people Tiny, the strongest kid Softie. Bones was no lightweight! Hardly skin and bones. A one-eyed cattle cross he was.

On Monday morning assemblies, as we were standing there on the asphalt in all weathers, shifting weight in crooked lines, Bones would follow Slade and sit erect beside the flagpole. No assembly hall then. Slade would strike his tuning fork against the pole, and sing or hum a quavering note, holding God in painful middle C, and a hundred raggedy boys would sing the anthem in not-so-sweet soprano, 'God save our gracious queen', no music to keep us in tune, some of us lithping through our missing teeth. And Slade would go puce unfurling the flag, while Bones with tilted head would yowl his own allegiance to the queen. And as we chanted the pledge, 'I honour my God, I serve the queen, I salute the flag,' Bones would often continue with his musical rendition. He was the most vociferous performer among us.

If the teachers sent us to Slade for some misdemeanour, our fate would rest entirely with Bones, who lay beside the desk like a sentinel with his head on his paws, and his one good eye like a laser on the door. We had to greet them both as we entered, before we were called upon to account for our misdeeds, and we never thought it strange. And woe betide the boy who snubbed old Bones in his fretful sleep.

We'd stand before the desk in dread, fearing what was in store for us, praying that Bones wouldn't stir. So should we punish them Bones? a placid Slade would ask, and if Bones emitted any sound, it didn't have to be a muted bark, it could be a clearing in his throat, or a passing of wind as he was especially prone to do, then Slade would unlock his cupboard and reach for a cane.

History has taught me that people can accept anything. Looking back it seems bizarre, but it was part of the scheme of things, and we didn't question it. Probably assumed that every school was the same. Adults are amazingly, even frighteningly resilient. Look at the conflict between nations, and between ordinary people. We adapt to anything. Little kids are even more malleable. We didn't know what normal was.

*

I don't remember an honours board in the foyer, or anywhere else, but it was sixty years ago, and I was only a kid. Looking at it is eerie, gold letters on the wooden panel that dull with subjugated time, the ghosts of ages past that prey on my kindled sentiment. Woods, Malone, Crowley, Gallagher, Stephenson, all principals since my time, but Slade is there too. His own little snatch of history. He'd be long gone now.

And I don't remember the honours board for the school captains. No wonder! The dates start after I left, and there are girls' names. A boy and a girl captain. The dux. There used to be a separate boys' and girls' school or campus on the same site, and never the twain did meet, except in kindergarten. Different buildings, different classes, even different playgrounds. We had the same recess and lunch times, but there was a yellow line painted up the middle of the asphalt to divide the playing areas. Boys on one side and girls on the other. And no fraternising. Not even talking.

Jennifer something. Jennifer Wrigley, that's it! Can't recall if we spoke, but we had a race the length of that yellow line, each on our own side of it, from the building to the fence and back. So I suppose someone must have arranged it. Jennifer was hauled off by the female teacher on playground duty and taken to the girls' mistress. I waited all day in trepidation that I would be called for and punished, but I wasn't.

I'll have to tell Oliver about that when I go to his classroom. He'll be amused. If you think your pa is a bit strange, I might say, if you think he has problems with Grandma or your mum, it's because he was taught to steer clear of girls. Even talking to them was thought to be unhealthy, or dangerous. The powers that be, must have had a jaundiced view of the perils of co-education.

And yet when I was in sixth class, the teachers organised folk dancing with the fifth class girls. So there was some concession from the school curriculum that sanctioned touch as well. It must have been a syllabus regulation that we prepubescent boys and girls interact before our hormone spree consigned us all to heterosexual hell. I thought it was wonderful. Poor sex-starved little boy!

Two close-together concentric circles were painted on the asphalt, with a diameter of four or five metres, and whichever class arrived first spread out around one of the circles and waited in ordered silence for their partners. For me, it was usually Narelle or Sylvia. I hoped the boys would be first to arrive, so I wouldn't have to pick and incur the disappointment of one of them. It was nice to think that each of them hustled her way around the circle to get to me first. Of course other boys and girls had their favourites, and devised ways of ensuring they met with their choice. On the odd occasion, a teacher insisted that we keep our positions as we moved in file around the circle. Then it was pot luck.

No girl wanted to dance with Fatty Burrell, and if there were more boys than girls, there'd be a scramble for partners to avoid being partnered by one of the female teachers. That was the height of embarrassment, and even worse than being partnered with another boy. I remember little Timmy Hutchins bursting into tears when Mrs Chadwick grabbed his hand. Red-faced, he could hardly put one foot in front of the other, and had to be half dragged into the dance.

The music with its ample share of static blared from loudspeakers, and we followed the teacher's example. We sensed something a bit intimate when Mr Smithers danced with Miss Byrne, but for us it was hardly 'dirty dancing', and a far cry from the freedom of modern dancing, though I can't recall exactly what we did. Probably something like the Canadian Three-step. Steps forward. Steps backwards. Turns. I can remember, though, the delicate, cool hands of Narelle and Sylvia, and the accidental brushing of our bodies.

Narelle was my girlfriend, or at least her girlfriends said so. I imagine young girls still pride themselves on their ability to promote romantic causes whether or not evidence justifies such promotion. If they're not interested in the boy themselves, that is. Sometimes I'd meet Narelle at the school gate on the way home. I'm sure it was arranged for us. I wouldn't have had the courage to do so. I'd have sooner been struck dead than admit to some special devotion. Our meetings were fleeting and usually wordless as there were buses to catch, though sometimes I'd hand her a conversation lolly. They were flat, coloured sweets, circular or heart-shaped, about the size of a fifty-cent piece with a printed two or three word message. Of course the message carried little meaning. 'Sweet Sixteen' meant nothing to the eleven year-old giver, or the ten-year-old receiver. It was the act of giving.

I'd either secrete my prize gift, purchased that morning, in my pocket, and risk the grit or fluff it might gather, or I'd try to hold it throughout the afternoon in my hand and hope that the heat and moisture generated didn't turn my gift into a sweating tablet. Wouldn't the kids of today laugh at our 'relationship', nominal, wordless and immaculate?

Can you imagine the script? Well, what did she say to you? Nothing. What did you say to her? Nothing. What did you do together? Nothing. All right, how did she look at you? Sorry?

Slade's great passion was the school band, the pride of Eastcliff Boys' Primary School, a swarm of flautists, four kettle drums and a bass drum. He was our tutor and I'm sure he looked favourably on us band members. We'd play at local community events, dressed in navy wool shorts, long socks, white shirt with a red tartan sash, and a peaked woollen hat with the school crest.

We played in school band competitions, and at the opening of the

Eastcliff railway subway, at which I managed to disrupt proceedings by fainting in the midst of interminable outdoor speeches. I was upstaged, though, by a second class boy who left a cider-coloured puddle at his feet. Every morning, the band assembled and played the boys into their classrooms from the morning assembly. Marching was mandatory until the building was entered.

What would Slade think if he saw the schools of today? Good old Slade. What was the name of his dog? And whatever has happened to all those bright-eyed boys and girls, pale-faced, innocent, stepping hand in hand, discreetly distanced in their inaugural dance of life? And what of Narelle, and S…Sally…whatever…

'Mr Ellis, you can go to Oliver's classroom now, if you like.'

*

'Do you know, Miss Gibbs, I was a student at this school once, and I sat in this very classroom. Third class. I think in the front seat here.' I avoid saying it was well before she and perhaps her parents were born, but I am hoping for some special recognition or at least surprise.

'I'll bet it's very different now,' she answers almost dismissively, an older man's nostalgia commonplace, before another grandparent competes for her attention. But what more could she say, after all?

Why do I feel this need to profess the swim of lapsing years, to admit some mite of ownership with all who come here now? Surely I can't feel dispossessed. It's very different. Is that all she can say? But how could she possibly understand the way I live its timeless legacy, how it's shaped my life's domesticated tutelage.

Oliver is so attentive. I have every reason to be proud as he takes me around the classroom. When he's finished, he's going to show me his workbooks. How lucky he is to have all of this. He's pointing out everything and we're moving around. There's a reading corner with large colourful cushions on the floor and shelves of plastic-covered books, a computer station I can only see properly by bending to avoid a display of children's artwork pinned to overhead strings, some comic mobiles, a long shelf beneath the window where the children can fetch their various named books from pigeonholes, and around every wall a panoply of richly laminated aids that defies routine austerity. All a far cry from the serried rows of crammed-in wooden desks that you never left until a bell rang, and with the only adornment a portrait of the queen.

There's a pealing coming from somewhere. Ah, I know, it must be Susie Parker, little Susie Parker with the heavy brass bell she collects from the office several times a day, and wields with her tiny hands like Rustum's sword. It must be time for our bottled milk. Hopefully it hasn't warmed too much in the crates. It'll still be drinkable if Stevie Dowd has stopped the magpies pecking at the tinfoil tops, especially the blue ones. Why do they go for the blue?

Ink monitor today. Yes, second Tuesday of the month. It's time for me to fill the inkwells and check all the pens, see that the nibs aren't bent. Make sure there's plenty of blotting paper. It's also my task to report any new scarrings in the wood, like Ronnie's carving of a penis on Giuseppe's desk that was reported to Miss Simpson, who wanted to know what it was. I hope there aren't any, because I don't like being a dobber.

Another bell. It must already be time to come back in.

'Pa, Grandpa!'

'I can hear you, Oliver. I'm not deaf. You don't have to tug at my sleeve like that.'

'But Grandpa.'

'Hang on a second, mate.' I must try to keep from being irritated. It must be obvious I have things to do. Can't he see that? The grandkids can be so persistent sometimes. 'I have to find my flute to help the children march back into class. Have you seen it? George'll be waiting out there with the old bass drum. Slade will want to know where I am. Be a good boy, Oliver, and dash out there and ask him if it's "The British Grenadiers" or "D'Ye Ken John Peel".'

# Climax

In a few minutes, they'll be entirely naked. They're already lying on the bed in a state of partial undress, fondling each other. So who are they, and why, apart from the obvious, are they here? 'Here', by the way, is her bedroom. Their names are Nigel and Amity, twenty-one and twenty respectively, both university students, and both regarded by their peers as a little different.

Difference sometimes struggles to reveal itself. There are times when it's obvious, when for instance someone is physically very different from the average, or when a person is demonstrably peculiar, someone with more than the usual share of idiosyncrasies. Perhaps someone who is unusually extroverted, or morose.

That isn't the case with Nigel and Amity. It's subtler than that. It's the sort of difference that others readily acknowledge, about which there is consensus, but if asked to define it, can only manage 'Well, it's hard to say, I don't know, just different.'

Amity lived in the family home with her parents and two younger sisters before she moved out early in the year to share a flat with a girlfriend. A free spirit, she found living at home oppressive. She went to a local private girls' school, and did particularly well. Even there, she acquired the reputation of being intuitive. Some called her a psychic.

On one celebrated occasion, there'd been a theft of valuable technological equipment from the school, and after the usual forensic examinations, and grilling of some of the more suspect students, Amity reported to the police that she could describe the culprit, and she reluctantly proceeded to do so in great detail. Her description resulted in an immediate arrest, and the inevitable questioning by the police, wondering how she knew, and whether to pursue her as an accomplice.

She was well enough liked at school, even by a clique of half a dozen girls who were known for being rebels, and who brought punishments on the heads of all. The teachers had a tactic of instilling responsibility in the girls by making the whole form share the penalty of any transgression. When Amity reported to a friend that she saw these girls defacing a wall mural in the school assembly hall, and asked if she should report them, the friend was shocked.

'No!' she said peremptorily, fearing payback from the girls. 'Have you lost your head?' She still remembers Amity's answer.

'No,' she said hesitantly, 'I don't think so,' and she reached up to test the whereabouts of her head.

Her friend thought it a great joke.

Nigel's supposed difference from others was as much physical as psychological. An only child, he still lived at home with his parents. He saw no reason to move out, and the doting attentions of his mother, with free board and lodging in his years of university study, overcame the need for a questionable freedom.

He did well at his all boys' school, and was well liked, even though he was interested in the more cerebral pursuits of chess and debating at which he excelled. While he was lean and fit, he didn't share the passion of his male peers for most sports, particularly the body contact sports, no doubt the legacy of injuries sustained in a car accident when he was a young teenager. The family had been on its way to a chess tournament at which Nigel was representing the school. His father, who was driving, sustained serious injuries in the collision. The other driver was drunk, and driving a four-wheel drive that veered onto the wrong side of the road. Fortunately, his mother was not hurt, but Nigel was hospitalised for quite some time, and had to catch up when he returned to school.

Other boys shared his reluctance for the more physical games, yet when his peers were asked why Nigel was different, his lack of interest in the rough and tumble of boys' sports didn't seem to be a factor. They couldn't provide a meaningful answer. 'I don't know,' they'd say. 'He's a good bloke, but somehow, well, he just doesn't fit the mould.'

\*

They're still on the bed partially clothed. They're talking softly and caressing more deliberately. Desire hasn't reached the point yet when it escalates into something more urgent, but it isn't far away. There's still time.

Every relationship is of course unique both in its expression and the way it evolves. That said, there is a general process that applies to most relationships between a man and a woman: an initial meeting, a decision to extend that meeting beyond the first superficial contact, the slow incremental give and take – revelations and concessions often involving admitting to vulnerabilities, and intimacy whether it be physical or not. It was no different for Nigel and Amity.

They met at a chess tournament and were drawn to play each other. The result was a stalemate, and they later enthusiastically critiqued each other's tactics. Considering themselves on an intellectual par, their discussion revealed other similarities and shared talents, and so they arranged to meet.

The relationship was slow to develop, as they were both shy and inexperienced, but that was another quality in common that brought them closer. They were able to share their personal histories and, after a few weeks, the close-to-the-bone truths that are rarely disclosed and that bond each other in the telling.

As they both became known to a wider set of friends, some of whom had labelled one or the other of them different, they were seen to be an ideal couple, perhaps because they both possessed the same indefinable difference. Nigel and Amity also felt this bond, and saw it as something to be proud of rather than regret.

There were the usual ups and downs in the relationship, and even a brief separation. The given reason was trivial, as most are. There are the big reasons like physical abuse, drug addiction and betrayal, but most are spurious excuses for some more pervasive feeling of disillusionment. She spoke harsh words. He was silently morose. He said he wondered what had attracted him in the first place. She said she doubted whether she had ever loved him. She threatened to leave. He told her to do so. Yet despite the hurt inflicted by both, there was no final ultimatum. The door was still open.

In every affair of the heart, there are times when that initial dramatic communion is fractured. That first promise or expectation is so great, so ideal, that it can't tolerate even the smallest flaw. The initial commitment has been so total, and the dream so absolute. And so the lovers are returned to the longing they experienced before they met, and the emptiness they feel leads to resentment, even open hostility or retreat. But the loneliness, and the thoughts of what they once enjoyed, soon becomes intolerable to them, and they come together again, often with greater conviction. So lovers' quarrels become a renewal of love. This was how it was for Nigel and Amity. And the result was a wolfish sex hunger.

*

They are still partially naked, now lying, and grappling on the bed with increased ardour. It hadn't been planned this way. Her flatmate's holiday provided the circumstance. Their recent separation and intensified confession of feeling for each other provided motive, or desire.

There was no doubt in the mind of either now about the inevitable conclusion. Each of them did wonder, then and later, how such strong sexual desire for the other could so easily defeat any trenchant argument they might previously have had against intimacy, and how easily it could ignore long-held convictions.

They'd come to the bedroom at once as soon as they entered her flat. They were of one mind. Embracing, they'd shuffled each other to the bed, and fallen on it together, still holding each other, and with their heads on the pillow. They held each other tightly and kissed more passionately than they'd been used to. They could feel the heat and texture of each other's body, and they longed for the trembling, potent secret of each other's sexuality. All was silent. The day was warm. The blinds were pulled, and the half-light allowed sight to excite touch.

That point of no return had arrived, the point at which emotion, or lust, informs reason. They peeled away their remaining clothes, unselfconsciously naked with each other for the first time, and readied their limbs for bodies' meld. It felt natural, and right. A faint slice of meddling light beneath the blind was lambent on her thigh.

But suddenly she gave a start to see him quickly sit up in the bed, remove his leg, and prop it up beside the bed. It stood upright by itself in tartan sock and shoe, a single leg without its torso. She felt the colour drain from her face. She hadn't known. It wasn't that she found it distasteful, a little disconcerting perhaps, but she needed time to adapt, a few seconds to get used to the idea.

A momentary resistance had followed her fright, or perhaps the unforeseen, but seeing his lack of concern, sitting upright in the bed, as though this were a very natural happening, she relaxed and allowed her emotion once again to swell to urgent need. Still supine on the bed, she gestured with open arms to welcome his attentions again.

But no sooner had he lain down against her and run his hand the length of her thigh than he sat up again, as if he'd just remembered something, this time shedding an arm complete with shoulder joint, a foot from his remaining leg, the non-caressing hand, and an eye. He placed them carefully on the floor beside the bed, each side of the leg, except for the eye that he placed on top of the digital alarm clock.

She didn't stay supine as he was doing this, but sat up in the bed, feeling somehow vulnerable, and now more than ever conscious of her sudden private nakedness that she proceeded to protect with her knees raised to her chin. She wondered what to say, and what she should do. Her ardour had cooled. She even felt a little squeamish.

Nigel noticed her discomfort – how could he not? – and felt a little aggrieved. He also understood her reaction, and began gently, appealingly. 'It's me you felt the urge to love, Amity,' he told her as she retreated, swinging her legs free of the bed.

'That might be true,' she replied defensively, 'but there's more of you on the floor than in the bed!'

Nigel swung his one footless leg over the side of the bed and sat beside her, taking her hand. 'What matters,' he told her, 'is a person's brain that enables them to think noble thoughts, solve great problems, decide how to help loved ones and pursue the truth, and their heart that makes them feel, be kind, compassionate and loving human beings, and live a life of purity devoted to another.'

Then he let go of her hand and, sensing her apprehension, decided that censure was the best approach. Though disappointed by her reaction, he still desired her. 'I really thought you were better than that,' he said. 'You've never been one to prize anything superficial. Am I just some object of your carnal needs? I don't think it's me you want at all, the quintessential me. If you're so concerned about this shell, this wrapping of flesh we call a body that conceals real meaning, perhaps you'd be happier with the beefcake at the gym!'

They remained sitting on the bed in silence, she feeling a little betrayed by his having kept her in ignorance when she thought she knew all his secrets, and he disguising a smidgen of guilt with an appeal to nobility.

After a few minutes, she relented and turned to him with soft and mournful eyes. Putting her arm around his shoulder, she whispered, 'Sorry, you're right,' and pulled him down into a lying position next to her on the bed.

As he felt his desire return in waves, he signalled his forgiveness with a tender look, and scanned her face to see if her desire was as great as his. As he did so, she deftly freed her head, and with both hands placed it on the bedside table facing towards them, where it observed his horror with the sweetest regard.